P
Carly Keene: Literary D_____ _____ _____ ntës

"Mix two parts adventure with one part literary history, add one spunky Alaskan girl, and you've got a fresh new series that puts the reader on the scene with *Carly Keene: Literary Detective*. In this first book of a series, Katherine Rue creates a rollicking adventure that takes readers from an island in southeast Alaska to the moors of England where the Brontë sisters are about to be inspired, Carly style. Not to be missed."

—**Debby Dahl Edwardson,** author of 2011 National Book Award Finalist *My Name is Not Easy*

"Young readers will be captivated by a gripping mystery that paints a vivid picture of 19th century England. Girls and boys will enjoy reading the adventures of this brave girl."

—**Ines Almeida,** CEO, Toward The Stars and Co-Executive Director, Brave Girls Alliance

"A captivating debut YA novel, and a great pick for mother-daughter book clubs."

—**Lori Day,** author of *Her Next Chapter*

"Loved this story. What a fantastic book! This story provides a great mixture of history and mystery. Worthwhile read for young girls."

—*Book Nerd*

"Younger audiences will find this book has plenty of action. After all, there are ghosts, time travel, mystery, and let's not forget adventure."

—*The Book Feed*

"I absolutely loved this story from the moment I opened the cover. This was a captivating read, especially for a debut author, and I can't wait to read the next installments of this series."

—**Melissa D'Agostino,** Librarian at Cecil College

BRAVING THE BRONTËS

KATHERINE RUE

In This Together Media
New York

In This Together Media Edition, 2014

Copyright © 2014 In This Together Media

Published in the United States by In This Together Media, New York, 2014

www.inthistogethermedia.com

BISAC:

1. Girls & Women- Juvenile Fiction
2. Time Travel—Juvenile Fiction
3. Ghost Stories—Juvenile Fiction
4. Historical (Europe)—Juvenile Fiction
5. Action & Adventure—Juvenile Fiction

ISBN - 978-0-9898166-3-2

eBook ISBN - 978-0-9898166-2-5

Cover Design and Illustrations by Nick Guarracino
Book Design by Makana Ching
Interior Layout and Ebook Design by Steven W. Booth

For Cedric, Jonathan, and Bryan—always;
and for Charlotte, Emily, and Anne

"Nan, was that you?" she asked.

Francesca didn't even twitch, already asleep. Carly peered out into the fog. Again she heard it.

"Save them."

Carly blinked hard, trying to see through the mist. *Nothing.* 5 a.m in Alaska during the summer meant it was light, but there was nothing to see. Carly shook her head. *I must be imagining things*, she thought. She curled up into her sleeping bag and was falling asleep when she heard a soft footfall next to the tent.

Her hand shot out to grab Francesca.

"Oh, my gosh, Francesca, there's someone out there!" she whispered.

"Wha—?" Francesca poked her head out of her sleeping bag.

"There's. Someone. Out. There." Carly whispered, with each word jerking her head toward where she'd heard the footsteps.

Francesca sat bolt upright. "Are you kidding me?!" she hissed. "What do you mean? Who could be out there? Are you sure it's not Lance?"

Carly's dog? Carly shook her head and mouthed, "Listen".

The two friends sat in their tent, barely breathing. The only sound they could hear through the damping mist was the gentle lap of tiny waves down the beach. Eventually, Francesca released Carly's arm and narrowed her eyes.

"You're nuts, and you woke me up at 5 a.m. to scare the pants off me. That's *not* tickety-boo."

Francesca was not at her best when you woke her up suddenly. Before Carly could protest, she retreated back into her sleeping bag and rolled over, facing away from Carly. Carly sat for a minute longer, listening, but all she heard were chatty sounds from a raven in the trees behind the tent. Eventually she lay down and closed her eyes.

The next thing she knew, Francesca was poking her in the ribs.

"I can't believe you woke me up in the middle of the night just to make me die of fright."

"I heard something whispering and walking by the tent, I swear. And it *was* tickety-boo," added Carly, using her and Francesca's favorite phrase. Carly's grandmother had learned it from her Scottish nanny and the two friends used it to mean everything from "wonderful" to "I-can't-believe-you-just-said-that," depending on the tone of voice. "Would you want me to let you sleep through something that exciting?"

"At 5 a.m.? Yes," said Francesca.

"Liar."

"Okay, fine, no. But next time you wake me up in the middle of the night, it better be a *real* adventure."

"It was real! Get up and I'll show you the footprints."

"Only if I get to be Nancy Drew."

"Good idea," said Carly. "I'll be Sherlock Holmes."

"We'll track that non-tickety-boo son-of-a-gun!" shouted Francesca, jumping out of the tent. Francesca didn't start the day with a bang, but once she woke up, she woke *up*.

A muffled groan came from the blue tent.

"I told you we should have made them camp at the other end of the island, George," came the voice of Carly's mother, Louisa. This was followed by another groan from Carly's dad.

"Can I start the fire? Carly and Francesca got to do it last night, so it's my turn." That was James, Carly's little brother.

"Doesn't everyone want to go back to sleep for a couple of hours?" asked Carly's dad in a hopeful tone.

"It's 6:30. I want to light the fire," said James.

Carly followed Francesca out of the tent at a more sedate pace. Lance, excited to see the family waking up, bounded out to greet the morning and everyone he could find.

"Morning. What're you doing?" James asked, looking at Carly, who was looking around suspiciously.

"Nothing," said Carly and Francesca at the same time.

James shrugged and ran off to dig matches out of the bags of gear. Carly led Francesca to the side of the tent, but found the beach grass trampled from the previous night's pre-bed adventures. Closer to the fire, the sand was too coarse to hold a footprint.

Francesca stopped even pretending to look for evidence halfway to the cooking area and went to watch James try to light the fire using only one match. Carly gave the ground one more cursory glance, then joined her. She and Francesca sat on a big driftwood log and watched James carefully build up the fire, starting with the kindling and a few tufts of dead grass he'd kept dry overnight under the rain fly of his tent.

"Did you *really* hear someone?" asked Francesca in a low voice.

Carly hesitated. Had she? It had been so early . . .

In her mind she heard the quiet footfalls outside the tent and shivered.

"Yeah, I did. It was super creepy. You would have loved it."

Francesca glanced behind them at the thick trees, which were such a dark green they looked almost black.

"Maybe it'll happen again," she said.

"Maybe," said Carly, not expecting anything of the sort. Adventures in real life were harder to come by than books always made it seem.

"Ha!" said James, standing up and looking at his fire in triumph. The flames licked cheerfully at the logs. "I am King James, lord of the fire!"

"More like King James the Annoying," said Carly.

"King James the Best Ever," countered her brother.

Before the scene devolved into an endless bout of name-calling, Francesca said they should all pick Narnia names.

"I want to be 'Queen Francesca the Brilliant,'" she said.

James could not be swayed from "James the Best." Carly finally settled on "Queen Carly the Brave."

Before James had finished scrambling into his rain pants (he made the critical error of thinking he could get the pants over his rubber boots and ended up hopping around on one leg trying to get his foot untangled), Carly and Francesca finished cleaning the dishes and set them on a driftwood log at the top of the beach to dry.

"You girls sure you don't want to come?" asked Carly's mom again.

"Yeah Mom, we're sure. We've got stuff to do here," said Carly.

Neither Carly nor Francesca thought it anyone else's business that they had decided to be shipwrecked princesses, lost on a deserted island. The plan had occurred to them the night before while they lay, staring up at the shadows of mosquitoes crawling on the tent. It stayed light so late at night during the Alaskan summer that it was hard to fall asleep right away. Of course, Carly's mom liked to say that they never stopped talking long enough to see whether they could fall asleep on time or not . . . but Carly and Francesca ignored such a poor-spirited remark.

Now a glance at one another confirmed the truth: With everyone but the royal hound out fishing, they would have the island to themselves. Perfect for a pretend.

"James, up you go," said Carly's mom, hoisting James over the bow of the boat. "Girls, don't forget to eat lunch if we're still out fishing when you get hungry."

"We won't forget," said Carly.

Carly's dad scrambled over the gunwale and went to stand ready with the motor while Carly's mom pushed the boat off the beach stern first. She waded out until the water almost came over her boots and then pulled herself up over the bow while Carly's dad lowered the motor. The girls waved goodbye and walked back up the gently sloping beach to take possession of the camp.

For a time, the two princesses sat in front of the fire, enjoying the quiet. Then they spent a while picking up driftwood and stacking it near the fire, because shipwrecked princesses didn't have people to make fires for them. They made another cup of cocoa with the hot water Carly's dad had put in a thermos before he left, and decided to walk all the way around the island to look for blueberry bushes.

As they called Lance, Carly felt the spot between her shoulder blades itch. It was as though someone was staring hard at her behind her back. She turned around sharply. *Nothing.*

"Come, Lance, come! Let's go for a walk!" shouted Carly.

At the word "walk," Lance bounded over.

"Good boy," said Francesca. "Find the blueberries, find 'em!"

"You're confusing the poor thing," protested Carly as Lance dashed first one way and then the other along the beach, trying to figure out what it was that Francesca wanted.

The feeling came again, more strongly this time.

"Francesca, there's someone watching us. I can feel it," said Carly in a sharp tone.

Francesca looked around, startled. She had thought the mysterious voice was one of Carly's pretends the night before and was unsure if her friend was still playing or not.

"For real? Where?"

"I think from the trees," said Carly, sidling closer.

Francesca and Carly stood shoulder to shoulder, staring at the woods. There was a long pause as they waited silently. Finally Carly spoke.

"Maybe we're giving ourselves the heebie-jeebies for no good reason."

"We do do that," agreed Francesca, but her tone was doubtful; she too had felt a sense of watchfulness upon them.

"Let's take Lance with us for protection," Carly said.

"Lance, come!" she and Francesca shouted together.

The girls resumed their walk. Between the rocks and the matted grass, it was slow going. The exertion made them hot and sweaty even though the weather remained grey and cool.

"Ugh, I don't think there are any blueberry bushes. Why did we think this was a good idea?" asked Carly when they were about a third of the way around the island.

"Because we're idiots," said Francesca, almost falling headlong over yet another slippery old log covered in dead grass.

Carly stopped to wait while Francesca pulled her left boot free. Lance was far ahead, only his tail visible above the grass.

In that instant, both girls froze at the distinct sound of rustling footsteps.

Francesca looked at Carly, her eyes wide. Carly looked at Francesca.

"What is that?" asked Francesca, gazing wildly around.

Carly sprinted towards the source of the rustling, but tripped in a tangle of old grass and fell. Francesca ran over to help her up.

"Dang, I almost got there in time!" said Carly, wiping her hands off on her jeans.

"Do you think it was the same thing you heard last night?" asked Francesca.

"The footsteps sounded the same. Oh, my gosh, can you believe we're having a real adventure?" Carly said.

"It might have been an otter or something," said Francesca.

"Nan. Come on." Carly gave her best friend a stern look. "You don't waste adventures like that. It was *not* an otter. Or any other animal." She paused. "Unless it was an animal sent with a message, to warn us of the quest we have to fulfill!"

Francesca, knowing that nothing short of an otter coming over and biting Carly on the ankle was going to make her admit this wasn't real, entered into the spirit of things.

"We'll probably have to take the skiff and rescue someone from one of the other islands where an evil enchanter has held them captive for hundreds of years."

"Or maybe the otter *is* the enchanted person—a nice wizard!" Carly said. "Good thing we didn't go fishing."

Abandoning their search for blueberries, the girls walked slowly back to camp, sometimes listening for more signs from enchanted wizard otters and sometimes describing the various tribulations and disasters which had resulted in an enchanted otter living for hundreds of years on a deserted island in Alaska.

When they returned, Carly piled more wood on the fire. Her stomach gave a loud rumble, reminding them it was time for lunch. No more footsteps had sounded, but the girls didn't let that stop them.

"Maybe the footsteps were aliens, with invisibility shields," suggested Francesca.

"No, not aliens with tons of technology—how could we do anything about them?" asked Carly. "There's no point in an adventure where the bad guys can zap you with phasers and disappear. How would we triumph and complete our quest?"

"Maybe *we're* aliens, and they're coming to tell us."

"Ohh, yes! I always thought I was a princess sent to be raised by common folk so I wouldn't be snobby, but aliens would be even better," said Carly.

"Maybe we're alien princesses. Two birds with one stone."

"Francesca, you're a genius."

While Francesca took a turn blowing on the new sticks, Carly squinted over the water, trying to make out the boat. She could see a speck that looked like it was the right shape, but it showed no signs of returning. She rummaged around in the cooler and pulled out some pilot biscuits, a big block of cheddar cheese, and some venison sausage. Beside her, Francesca peeled a couple of oranges and found the Oreo cookies.

"You're so lucky," she said. "My parents won't buy Oreos, not even for a camping trip."

"My mom always does this big sigh when we ask, but my dad talks her into it," said Carly. "Only for camping trips, though."

"I'm going to try and get my dad to do that," said Francesca.

"Make sure he says it's only for camping. Then she won't feel like she's breaking her Nutritional Rules." Francesca's mom had lots of Nutritional Rules. Carly had long ago decided to pretend she liked millet rather than try and think up excuses to avoid it when she was over at the Eriksons' for dinner.

"I'm not sure," said Francesca. Her mother's Nutritional Rules were a force to be reckoned with. "Does it always work?"

"Well . . . almost always. Unless Dad's just done something like buy Mom a chainsaw for Valentine's Day," said Carly.

Francesca and Carly started giggling—the story was a beloved family joke.

"What about the snow blower for her birthday?" added Francesca.

"She *liked* that one," said Carly. "Which goes to show that there is *no* romance in Alaska. How can anyone be swept off their feet by a snow blower?"

Francesca laughed. "I know. My parents were so excited when they redid the roof. They're crazy! We were definitely born in the wrong century, because we'd *never* find those things romantic."

"We are destined for epic romantic adventures," agreed Carly.

"So why don't you apply for that French camp your grandmother told you about?" asked Francesca. "It doesn't get much more romantic than horseback riding and speaking French on a gorgeous old plantation in Virginia!"

"I told you: I'm horrible at languages. It stinks."

"You're really good at school. I don't think you can be as bad as you think . . ." Francesca started, but Carly interrupted her.

"I really am. My parents even talked about getting me tested for it, since I'm so much worse at them than everything else."

Francesca gave her a gentle nudge on the shoulder. "Well, if it turns out we're alien princesses you'll probably get a universal translator thingy, so it won't matter."

Carly and Francesca sat by the fire, eating lunch and laughing about everything and nothing, the way best friends do, until they saw the skiff headed back in towards shore. James was waving wildly from the bow. As soon as they were close enough to hear, he started shouting, "We caught five fat coho!

Two of them were on at once! Dad says we don't have enough ice so we have to pack up and go home early or they'll spoil!"

Carly and Francesca looked at each other in dismay—they'd been counting on one more night out on the island. Even so, they waded down to catch the bow of the boat and hold it off the beach while Carly's mom lowered James into the shallow water.

"Do we have to?" asked Carly.

"I know you're disappointed, girls, but we listened to the marine radio and the weather's going to get worse as the afternoon goes on. Better to get back before the wind comes up."

"Let's get the camp packed up," said Carly's dad.

So Carly and Francesca helped strike tents, jam sleeping bags back into their waterproof stuff sacks, douse the fire, pile the bags on the beach, and ferry gear down to the boat. They kept half an ear out for any strange footsteps or voices, but nothing intruded on the bustle of activity.

Not long after the skiff returned from fishing, they were pushing off again, this time with everyone on board and ready (however reluctantly) to go home. Carly couldn't tell if the ghostly voice and footsteps had been real or part of her imagination—either way, it seemed as though they belonged to the island. The memory slipped away from Carly the closer she got to the harbor and home.

~ CHAPTER TWO ~

"It's not *fair*," groaned Carly several hours later. "Francesca and I were about to write a story about our thrilling adventures on the island! We don't have time to go buy more vacuum-packer bags for the fish."

"You and Francesca spend almost every day together," said her mother. "You can write your story tomorrow. Today I need you to walk to the store; your dad and I have to keep cutting up the salmon, or we'll be here all night. If you want to take James, you can."

"We can plan out the wizard's adventures while we walk," said Francesca.

"We're not taking James, though. I've heard enough about how hard the coho fought to last me the rest of my life," said Carly.

"That's fine. Get some money out of my purse and hurry back," said her mom.

In the mudroom, Carly struggled with her boots while Francesca idly turned over the piled-up mail. A glossy brochure caught her eye. Francesca pulled it out and read: "Located just outside Richmond, Virginia, St. Timothy's offers a US Pony Club-certified riding center combined with a French immersion camp." Over the picture of happy campers riding happy ponies was written in silver marker: "Carly, dearest, apply ASAP, will send plane ticket. xoxo Grandmother."

"What're you looking at?" asked Carly, swinging a canvas grocery bag over her shoulder.

"Holy smokes, you didn't show me the brochure! How could this *be* more perfect for you?" Francesca said, holding up the pamphlet.

"I thought we were going to plan our story," Carly murmured.

"We can do that later," said Francesca, waving a hand airily. "This sounds awesome, Carly! I wish I could go, too, but we're going to Minnesota for my mom's family reunion and then we have to help Granny on her farm. You *have* to apply!"

"But I told you, Nan, I'm bad at languages," said Carly, opening the door. "And horses are so . . . twitchy. I'd apply if it were a science camp."

"Maybe going to an immersion camp where all you do is practice French while riding adorable horses is what you need to be more confident," said Francesca in an encouraging tone. As the two girls walked down the street, she continued, "Like when I thought I would never be able to make the cross-country team but you helped me practice and I did."

"It's not the same, Nan—you just needed to learn how to pace yourself. I might have a learning disability," said Carly.

"Even if you do, that doesn't mean you shouldn't apply," said Francesca. "It sounds tickety-boo!"

"But . . ." started Carly, and then stopped.

"But what?" prompted Francesca.

"But . . . what if I don't get in?" asked Carly, pulling up the hood of her raincoat against the drizzle.

There was a pause.

"Why wouldn't you get in?" asked Francesca. She gave her friend a reassuring smile. "You're good at everything."

"Except languages," repeated Carly.

"We're only twelve. I think you have some time," said Francesca. "And, hey, what does that have to do with getting admitted? You're not supposed to be awesome at French. If you were, you wouldn't need French camp."

"I'll think about it," said Carly, opening the door to the hardware store. "But I don't want to talk about it anymore."

Francesca raised her eyebrows at Carly, but kindly stayed silent, knowing that bugging Carly would only make her more stubborn. The girls bought vacuum-pack bags and started back toward Carly's house, but they turned left out of the store so they could take the long way, past Juneau Coffee Co.

A lucky thing, as it turned out. One lucky thing in a series of lucky things.

For if Carly and Francesca had not read the right sort of books, they would never have turned down the little alleyway that appeared off of Seward Street that day. Where there was usually a weedy patch between a local bank and an art gallery, there appeared a tiny side street neither girl had ever seen before. As anyone who has read C. S. Lewis or E. Nesbit or J. K. Rowling knows, only dull, foolish children ignore mysterious alleyways that appear from nowhere. Carly and Francesca *could* have gone straight home with the vacuum-pack bags, as Carly's mother certainly expected. But they didn't.

For Carly and Francesca knew how to Recognize a Mystery when they saw one. Weren't they always creating Mysterious Circumstances for their own amusement? This time, it wasn't in their imaginations, and they weren't pretending. It was right there. A street that appeared out of nowhere.

So they turned down it, and immediately the sense of being watched returned, stronger than ever.

"I thought we'd imagined it before," whispered Francesca.

"Shhh," said Carly. "But keep your eyes open."

It was too exciting to be on a real adventure at last. After all their imagining of what it would be like, it was finally happening! Almost without noticing, they held each other's hands in a tight grip.

Much to the two friends' disappointment, there did not seem to be anything happening on the mysterious lane. The rain was still drizzling down lightly, and there was a damp, chilly breeze. No magical beasts or castles were visible. In fact, the street was paved and had a sidewalk (albeit a cracked, skinny sidewalk), like any small city street might. There were not even any mysterious glowing doorways to go through, because it seemed the little street ran between the backs of buildings.

"What," said Carly, breaking the silence, "is the point of a Mysterious Lane if there isn't anything in it?" Her tone was equal parts disappointment and exasperation.

"Look!" said Francesca, pointing ahead on their left.

Not all the walls were blank—one narrow doorway hunched in between two jutting posts. While it could not be accused of beckoning anyone in with cozy lights or delicious smells, Carly and Francesca hurried over and stood, staring. The door handle was an old-fashioned thumb latch. Carly put out a hand and touched it lightly.

"This is the best thing that's ever happened. I *knew* we were born for adventure," said Carly, almost breathless with excitement.

Francesca nodded. "Hurry up and open the door!"

Carly took a deep breath—there was no turning back from adventures once you opened the door to them—and pushed down the latch. A bell jangled somewhere in the back of the shop. Carly and Francesca looked at each other.

"Want to go first?" whispered Carly, raising her eyebrows.

Francesca nodded. She stepped through the door, Carly close behind.

The first thing she saw was a floor mat that said "Please Wipe Your Feet." So Francesca did, followed by Carly. They had read enough fairy tales to know you didn't start off wrong by ignoring polite requests.

Protocol observed, the two girls looked around. The rain-dim day could not hide that it was a very interesting place. Shelves and shelves of books met their delighted gaze. Shelves all the way up to the ceiling and all the way down to the floor. Shelves everywhere—the shop looked like a rabbit warren filled to bursting with books.

"Wow," said Francesca in an awed tone.

"Hello?" Carly called towards the back of the dim, dusty space. "Hello? Is anyone here?"

There was no sound except the pitter-patter of rain on the window.

"Let's look around," suggested Francesca.

Carly and Francesca walked along the shelves, looking at the books. Most of the bindings were leather and cracked. A few paperbacks were stuck in between the older books, but they were just as worn as the leather-bound books.

"None of these look new," Carly said.

"Do you recognize any titles?" asked Francesca.

Carly shook her head. Many of the books were in foreign languages. This wasn't anything like the bookshops they normally went to. She and Francesca knew all four of the local shops (two new and two used) well. In fact, Carly lived within walking distance of one of the new bookstores, and one of the used. From the time she was old enough to cross streets safely by herself, she'd been one of the shops' best patrons. She could spend hours looking through books, reading snippets, and sipping hot cocoa. Francesca often bemoaned the fact that she didn't live close enough to walk to any of the bookstores. She had to beg a ride from her parents or take the bus.

Caught up in looking at all the strange titles, the girls moved deeper into the shop. Soon they could no longer see the front door. Carly paused to look at a particularly fat volume whose gold leaf title had rubbed mostly off.

"I'm going to see if I can find an original copy of *The Ordinary Princess*," said Francesca. "The new editions leave out all the color illustrations."

Carly nodded absently. "It seems safe enough. I'll be along in a second."

As Carly wandered up and down the aisles, trailing her hand along the spines of books as she went, she noticed a faint glow towards the back of the shop. She hesitated. Should she go see what it was? Or should she find Francesca so her friend didn't miss a single moment of the adventure?

"Francesca?" she called. No answer. But then, Francesca was notorious for not hearing what anyone said to her when she was concentrating.

Carly decided there was no harm in going to look without waiting. She'd run and grab Nan the second something interesting happened.

But, coming around the last bookcase, she was disappointed to see that the light came from nothing more exciting than a fire in an old-fashioned fireplace. Two comfy looking armchairs stood on either side.

"Hello?" Carly called.

"Ah, yes, hello. Let me see, hmm . . . no, no, that can't be right," said a distracted-sounding voice.

From the dark corner to the right of the fireplace, a door opened and a small, bent old man bustled out, looking at something he carried carefully in both hands.

"Errrr, what can't be right?" Carly asked.

The old man looked up in surprise. "The binding on this first edition is supposed to be *blue*, I'm sure of it. Not red. Really, they can't expect me to believe it's supposed to be *red*!"

"First edition of what?" Carly asked, trying to get a look at whatever he was holding.

"*Jane Eyre*, of course. What else would I be talking about? And why haven't you sat down yet?" he replied, gesturing to one of the armchairs.

Carly looked at him in surprise.

"Well, for one thing, you haven't invited me to," she said.

"How can you expect to look at an extremely rare and valuable old book if you aren't sitting down properly? What are children coming to these days? And here, wear these archival gloves so the oils on your fingers don't hurt the pages," he added, holding out white cotton gloves.

This was not the sort of adventure Carly had been counting on when they started down the mysterious alleyway. She loved books, but having strange old people insist she sit down and put on gloves before looking at a book she'd never read did not sound fun. She wondered if she should mention that she hadn't had time to change out of her camping clothes, so her pants might be grubby. *I just won't put the book on my lap*, she thought. *And where is Francesca? This is kind of weird. Not scary, but definitely weird.*

"I told my dad we would walk the dog as soon as we got home . . ." she said.

The old man snorted. "I offer her a look at the first edition of *Jane Eyre*, and she wants to walk the dog. No imagination, these children."

That stung. If there was one thing Carly knew she had plenty of, it was imagination. Who was the one who thought up a new religion to tempt the snow gods into giving them a good ski season last winter by sacrificing carrots carved with faces? *Me!* she thought indignantly. Who invented a secret code to write notes with her best friends? *Me!* Who invented a new kind of cake, one that was all blue? *Me!* Well, to be fair, the cake had been dense and hard and even she only wanted one piece . . . but still. Carly had plenty of imagination, and she knew it.

Carly plopped down in the chair to the left of the fire and glared at the old man. He chuckled.

"Got a bit of fire in you. Good to see. What's your name?"

Carly hesitated. She did not like her name. As she had pointed out on numerous occasions, it was unfair of her parents to have given her an unromantic nickname for a proper name. Francesca had a name that belonged to a heroine from a novel—as Carly had often told her friend. Who ever heard of a romantic or plucky heroine named *Carly*? Even her middle name didn't help—Leigh. Carly Leigh? That just made her sound like she had a stutter. Still. It was hers, and she couldn't do anything about it.

"Carly. Just Carly," she said and held out her hands for the white gloves.

"Well, Carly-just-Carly, I've got small hands so the gloves should fit," the old man said. "What I'm about to show you isn't any old first edition of *Jane Eyre*, although those are rare enough. This one supposedly belonged to Charlotte Brontë herself."

His pleased look faded as he started to mutter again about the binding, but Carly wasn't paying attention. She'd heard of *Jane Eyre*, but her mom thought she was too young to read it. Carly sometimes suspected her mom said that just to make sure Carly would want to read a book *immediately*, but she didn't mind. Her mom had good taste. She hadn't gotten to *Jane Eyre* yet, though.

"Why isn't it in a museum?" she asked.

"Eh? Museum? Oh, it will be," the old man said.

Carly liked the idea of getting to hold and look at something that was going to a museum. The worst part of museums was that you were never allowed to touch the interesting things in them. She drew the gloves on, taking a moment to admire how neat and old-fashioned her hands looked—like Meg in *Little Women*, she thought.

"Are you done admiring yourself?" asked the old man in a dry tone.

Carly flushed.

"Yes. May I look at the book now?"

"Very well. Always support the spine in one hand, and gently turn the pages with the other. It's fragile, you know."

Carly held out her hands, feeling nervous. The book settled into her palm with a steady weight. She gingerly curled back in the chair and opened the front cover. The words, *Jane Eyre: An Autobiography, Edited by Currer Bell*, stared back at her.

"I thought you said Charlotte Brontë wrote this?" Carly asked.

"She did. All three Brontë sisters used pen names: Currer, Ellis, and Acton Bell for Charlotte, Emily, and Anne Brontë."

Carly carefully turned the pages, past the *Introduction*—introductions were boring—to the first page of the story.

Firelight flickered over her face as she pored over the book. Entranced, she didn't notice when the old man gave a satisfied smile and went back through the doorway out of which he had so suddenly appeared. She forgot that Francesca was somewhere about, and she didn't notice the fire roaring up brighter and hotter.

She didn't notice the fire, but its heat made her sleepy, and as she got to the sentence, "It contained a bookcase: I soon

possessed myself of a volume, taking care that it should be one stored with pictures," the letters started to blur and she couldn't keep her eyes open. Carly's head drifted down to her chest, and

25

her hands, still carefully holding the book, drifted down to her lap.

A hand on her shoulder shook her gently awake.

"Come along, Miss Caroline, you'll ruin your eyes reading by the fire like that, and Miss Brontë says it's time for your tea."

Carly sat up and looked around. An elderly servant in a long black dress and a white cap stood in front of her. While she was still sitting in a chair in front of a fire, it was not the same chair, and it was not the same fire. Nothing about the room was the same, except Carly.

She looked down at herself, and found that while she was still wearing the white gloves, she was also wearing a dress with a—was that a *pinafore*? What had happened to her? Carly stared at the maid in stupefied silence. Where had the book-shop gone? Where was Francesca? Was this a dream?

"The tea is getting cold. Do come along; Miss Brontë is waiting," said the woman, gesturing impatiently towards the door.

Unsure of what else to do, Carly stood and followed her out of the room.

When she looked back from the doorway, she could have sworn the fire winked at her.

ᔕᎧ Chapter Three ᔕᎧ

Had the servant said that *Miss Brontë* wished her to drink tea? Carly stuck a finger in her ear and wiggled it. She must have heard wrong.

The woman led Carly across a hall and into another room. Carly stopped short on the threshold: The room was full of people—an older man, three young women, and a moody-looking younger man.

"Ah, there you are, Caroline. I am pleased you take your studies so seriously, but try to remember that punctuality is also a virtue," said the oldest of the three women, gesturing for Carly to take a seat next to her on the settee. "Thank you for finding her, Tabby."

Carly still didn't move. She was too amazed to do more than stand, gaping.

"Mouth closed, Caroline. What is wrong with you this afternoon? I wish to instruct you in how to pour tea, something every lady needs know." The woman gestured again to the seat next to her.

"I—I beg your pardon, but—what?" gasped Carly, looking around wildly for the old bookseller or Francesca, for anything at all familiar.

"Really, Charlotte," said the thinnest and palest of the women. "She seems ill. Are you ill?" she asked Carly.

"I didn't think so," said Carly, touching her forehead. It didn't feel hot, but her mom always said you couldn't feel if your own forehead was feverish.

Wait, she thought. *That woman just called her Charlotte. Miss Brontë . . . Is that Charlotte Brontë? Am I going crazy?*

"Then stop dilly-dallying and go help Charlotte pour the tea," said the third and tallest of the women.

"Yes, I for one am dying of thirst over here," said the younger man.

"Please take off your gloves, Caroline. There is no need to wear them in the house, you know," said Charlotte.

Carly looked down, stunned. She wasn't sure what to do—these people, these Brontës, obviously thought she was someone named Caroline, but she had no idea how she could be standing in a room with Charlotte Brontë and what looked like her whole family. Everyone was staring at her, so Carly took the seat indicated by Charlotte, her mouth still half open in astonishment.

"Mouth closed, Caroline. I dislike repeating myself. Pouring tea is the duty of the hostess at any gathering, and now that you are getting older, you will be expected to help your mother. When she returns, that is," said Charlotte.

"Returns?" said Carly.

"Oh, my dear, you mustn't worry that she and your father will not return!" exclaimed the pale woman. "I am sure that your father's business in India cannot take more than a year to complete, and with the journey home you may depend on seeing them before two years have passed."

"What?" said Carly, still trying to understand the startling turn her adventure had taken.

"Anne, I too am sure Caroline's parents will return without incident. However, that is neither here nor there. Caroline, watch me as I ready cups for my father and Branwell. You see how one first warms the cups with hot water, then discards the water into this bowl . . ."

Carly stopped listening. So this Caroline's parents were either in India or on their way there—that didn't help her figure out what had just happened. And what about Francesca? They were supposed to be having this adventure together!

She tuned back into the conversation in time to hear the older gentleman—apparently the father of the others—request extra sugar in his tea.

"I know sugar is dreadfully expensive, but I am an old man and have developed something of a sweet tooth," he said. Charlotte added an additional lump and gestured impatiently to Branwell, indicating he should take the tea to their father. Branwell made a sulky face, but got up and carefully placed the cup and saucer next to the old man.

"Here you are, Father. I've set it on the table," he said.

"I can see that. I'm not completely blind, you know," said the father grumpily.

The old man put out a hand hesitantly and picked up his tea cup. Carly watched in fascination as he took a sip and set the cup down precisely in its saucer. *He looks as though he's practiced*, she thought. Branwell came back to collect his own cup of tea and slouched back to his seat. Carly eyed him with interest. She had just been complaining to Francesca about not having an older brother, and here one was, ready for the adopting. She was about to ask him if he had always wanted a much younger sister to whom he could teach life lessons and introduce adventure when Charlotte recalled her attention.

"Caroline, please bring these to Anne and Emily—and be careful not to spill."

It was difficult to carry two full cups of tea without spilling into the saucers, and Carly walked slowly. Emily merely nodded her thanks, but Anne smiled at her and said, "While it must be considered unusual for a wife to accompany her husband to India, I am sure it is perfectly safe with the Hindoos so well governed by the East India Company—I believe they have completely stamped out that dreadful cult of Thuggery."

"Yeah, I'm sure they'll be fine. My mother's very hearty, you know," said Carly, wondering what a cult of Thuggery might be.

Anne's mention of her mother made Carly feel less ecstatic about being in the middle of a mysterious adventure. What if her family and Francesca knew she was gone and worried about her? Another thought nearly made her dump tea into Anne's lap. What if she was stuck here forever?

Carly handed off the tea cup before she made a mess and tried to comfort herself with the thought that in most books she'd read, the people left behind never knew anything had happened to the heroine while she was having her adventure—like Lucy in Narnia. Plus the heroine always got back home at the end of the book.

But that was much less comforting now that she was the one to whom the adventure was happening.

Carly hardly had time to burn her tongue on an incautious sip of tea and ponder the complexities of time-travel (if this weren't a dream—which Carly more than half believed it to be), before Charlotte had her up again, this time handing out scones. Being the hostess seemed like a lot of work to Carly. When did *she* get to eat a scone? Emily had already scarfed down two. Would it be polite to grab the last one off the tray before someone else got to it?

Before tea was over Carly had managed to eat and had helped Charlotte tidy the dirty cups and saucers on the tea tray.

"I believe we will take a turn in the gardens while the weather continues fine, Caroline. The light will not go for an hour yet, and we can discuss your studies," said Charlotte.

Carly, still not used to being called Caroline, looked over her shoulder to see who Charlotte was talking to. But there was no one behind her, and Charlotte was definitely standing by the door, waiting for Carly to join her. Why was she here, and with Charlotte Brontë of all people? Carly had pictured adventures involving more sword fighting or magic wand waving and less tea drinking.

Giving a mental shrug and recalling that in all the adventures she'd read about everything became clear in time, Carly followed Charlotte to the hallway, where Charlotte handed her a woolen coat. The two went out the front door, following a path around to the side of the house and into a formally laid out garden that showed signs of long neglect. It must be autumn, Carly thought, noticing how what sunlight there was held little heat, and how the flowers were mostly done blooming. A cool wind blew. She perked up her ears when Charlotte started talking.

"You have been here a week, so tomorrow we will begin your formal schooling. I am relieved to have a pupil who, for once, is not a dolt."

Carly didn't know what to say to that, but was interested to hear that even though "Caroline" had been in this house a week, Charlotte and the others appeared to see no difference between whoever she was before and Carly.

"I have decided your mornings will be devoted to the study of history and geography, while the afternoons will be for literature, French, and German."

"Oh, no!" Carly's stomach dropped at the thought of having to try and learn *two* foreign languages. She was awful at one! Charlotte ignored the interruption.

"When you have made satisfactory progress, we shall add Latin. At least one half hour a day will be given to practicing the pianoforte and we will add in drawing as the weather permits," she said.

When Carly's mother had insisted that she and her brother James take piano lessons, she had said, "It might be useful later." Carly was pretty sure her mom hadn't meant, "In case you ever are magically transported somewhere you need to play the piano so they don't know you're from a different time."

Nevertheless, Carly made a mental note to thank her mother for the piano lessons next time she saw her.

"What about math and science?" asked Carly, "I was just saying to Francesca that I prefer science to languages. Is she here too? Francesca, I mean?"

She stopped when she realized Charlotte was staring at her in apparent horror.

"No? There's not another girl here, about so tall, with black hair . . ."

"I do not know to whom you are referring. And while not a usual subject for a gently bred lady, it might be possible to eventually include some study of mathematics beyond basic arithmetic," said Charlotte. "But my scientific knowledge does not extend past a smattering of botany. Anything more is not fit for a young lady."

"Oh, whatever. I like all the subjects," said Carly hastily.

"I am glad," said Charlotte, looking around the garden and sighing.

Carly wasn't sure what the appropriate response was when one's apparent governess sighed while out walking, and so looked about her in silence, too. The house was a large stone one with two stories. The garden they walked in flanked it on the right side. Carly glanced behind her and saw through a belt of trees gentle hills stretching away into the distance.

Charlotte saw her look and said, "*I dream of moor, and misty hill / Where evening closes dark and chill . . .* " She paused, and added with a slight smile, "Well, not so chill yet. But it soon will be."

"Was that poetry? Who wrote it? What's a moor?" asked Carly. She'd read about moors in books like *The Secret Garden*, but had no clear idea what they were.

"The moor is all the open, wild land you saw as you came here. It is covered with heather and broom and I believe more beautiful than any more cultivated fields," said Charlotte. She hesitated before she continued, "My sister Emily wrote the lines. We recently published a book of poetry . . . to very little effect, I'm afraid." A bitter crease appeared at the corners of her mouth.

"But what about . . . " Carly stopped herself before she said, "What about *Jane Eyre*," because it occurred to her that if Charlotte had published the book as Currer Bell it might be hard to explain how Carly knew Charlotte had written it. *Probably mess up the space-time continuum*, thought Carly. So she changed her first sentence into a coughing fit and asked: "I think it's very nice. May I see more of it some time?"

"Yes, it's not as though anyone else is clamoring to read it," said Charlotte. "But enough. We should return inside and you may practice the piano for half an hour before dinner and bed."

"Oh, goody," Carly muttered very, very quietly under her breath.

Inside, Carly was shown to the piano upstairs in what Charlotte called "the school room that used to be our study as children," given music, and left to her own devices.

"Emily is the best pianist, but she is helping Tabby make dinner and cannot be spared to give you a lesson right now," said Charlotte as she went to help her father write letters.

The room with the piano was not as cheerful (or warm) as the dining room, and Carly played half-heartedly through some Mozart. She was a competent but not brilliant pianist, for she liked doing too many other things to practice as much as her music teacher would like. Besides, she was too busy turning over the events of the afternoon in her mind to notice or care about the occasional wrong note or incorrect fingering. This *must* be a dream, she thought, but it felt very real (she even pinched herself to be sure). How and why had she appeared in this place? She did not reach any conclusions before being summoned to dinner.

When she got downstairs, she found the whole family seated and surprised herself by eating a very hearty meal.

Francesca always said that heroines lost their appetite when faced with peril. Carly had no intention of meeting any peril on an empty stomach. Surely it would become obvious in the morning what she was doing here—if she didn't wake up in her own bed at home—so she ate the roast beef, the peas, the potatoes, and was almost too full for the stewed apples.

During the meal, Carly noticed Branwell drank quite a lot of wine, and she caught Charlotte exchanging looks with Anne as he poured himself yet another glass—much the way Carly's Great-Aunt Cynthia always did at family reunions. Perhaps Branwell could be the older brother she reformed, Carly thought. Then he'd be eternally grateful and introduce her to his most handsome friend.

The most conversation Carly had during the meal was when she asked about the sound of the wind outside—it had gotten more noticeable during dinner. A particularly loud gust, one that made the fire belch smoke into the room, prompted her to ask,

"Is a storm coming? The wind sounds so wild."

Emily gave a mirthless chuckle.

"You'll know if the wind truly starts wuthering. The moors do not suffer fools lightly."

CARLY KEENE: LITERARY DETECTIVE

Unable to tell if Emily was calling her a fool, Carly ventured no more remarks on the weather.

After dinner she was sent to bed (at 7 p.m., an unreasonably early hour—her bedtime at home was 9 o'clock!) Thankfully, Charlotte took her upstairs to help her unbutton the pinafore buttons at her back, under her dress, so Carly didn't have to ask her way to a bedroom she'd supposedly been sleeping in for a week.

Looking around, she realized that she was most certainly not the bedroom's only occupant. There was a woman's dress folded over the back of a chair and two hairbrushes on the dresser. Her uneasy suspicion that she would be sharing the bed was confirmed when Charlotte left her with a candle and the words, "I expect you shall be asleep by the time I come up. Pleasant dreams."

Alone, Carly stood in the center of the room for a long minute. She'd shared beds at sleepovers with friends before—Francesca had practically moved into her bedroom the summer before when her parents were out of town a lot, but a governess she had only met that day? What if Charlotte snored? What if *Carly* snored? What if she had to get up and use the outhouse? At least growing up in Alaska and camping had taught her important time-travel skills of this latter sort, Carly thought, profoundly thankful.

Maybe there was a trundle bed underneath the big bed? Carly bent down and looked. No. Just a chamber pot. Yikes, did they expect her to pee in front of her governess? She'd rather go outside in the bushes and freeze!

Firm in her determination, Carly decided to go back downstairs and ask to use the outhouse—surely they had one, as she hadn't seen a place for a proper bathroom. Leaving her pinafore on the bed but buttoning her dress back up, Carly walked out onto the dark landing and reached out a hand to feel for the banister.

She gave a muffled shriek and jumped backwards when her hand found not the railing, but a living arm. A drunken chuckle made her realize that it was Branwell.

"Oh! You scared me!" she said, her heart still racing.

"Did I?" asked Branwell, leaning heavily on the railing and blinking owlishly at Carly in the dim light filtering up from downstairs. "Why? Don't think I was planning to push you down the stairs. Were you?"

"Was I what?" asked Carly, backing up so that Branwell couldn't grab her.

"Planning to push me down the stairs?" His voice dropped to a mutter and he continued, "They could make it look like an accident. That's why I need the gun . . ."

"Gun?" Carly squeaked. Did this drunk guy have a *gun*?

Branwell refocused on Carly.

"What the devil are you doing out of bed?" he demanded.

"Nothing." said Carly, deciding even chamber pots were preferable to drunken madmen who raved about guns.

"Then get back in your room. And stay there," said Branwell, wagging a finger at Carly.

"Yes, sir," she said, backing slowly towards her bedroom door.

"And no pushing people down the stairs," added Branwell as Carly shut the door and leaned against it, hoping Branwell would not try to come in and lecture her further.

She heard his uneven footsteps cross the landing to the room across from hers and the slam of the door behind him. Carly undressed with trembling fingers. She'd never seen a drunk person before, and she decided she didn't like it. Branwell had seemed so . . . uncontrolled, so unreachable by words or reason. He was definitely *not* the older brother of Carly's imagination.

Hiding under the bedcovers, Carly listened to the wind blowing furiously around the house. What was the word Emily had used at dinner? Wuthering. It didn't sound like a real storm, but like someone moaning and crying outside the window.

"Stop it, Carly Leigh Keene!" she whispered fiercely to herself. "You are letting your imagination get the better of you. There is nothing out there, and the sooner you get to sleep, the sooner it will be morning. You know perfectly well that everything looks better in the morning. Maybe the weather will be nice. Maybe you'll be home."

Carly resolutely shut her eyes. Being in a strange world for a reason she did not know was much less fun in the dark—particularly with Branwell talking about guns and pushing people down stairs. And that wind outside her window *did* sound like some lost soul pleading to be let in. The wind at home, even when it was loud, never sounded so human or so frightening.

The best thing to do, Carly decided, was to fall asleep as fast as possible and stay that way till morning—when she would find herself back home or even in that odd bookshop. Carly told herself this firmly and repeated it a couple of times, for emphasis.

On the twentieth repetition or so, the exhaustion of trying to enjoy an adventure that was not at all what she had expected; of being brave and acting like the sort of heroine a "Caroline" should be; of realizing, with a sleepy smile, that she now had the name she'd always wished was hers . . .

In the midst of this mental muddle, Carly fell asleep with the covers pulled up over her head. The wind slowly died down and the same sense of expectant watching filled the room, but Carly slept on.

⮑ CHAPTER FOUR ⮌

Carly rolled over with a sudden "Mmmph!" that woke her up. For a second, she lay buried under the covers; then her nose told her that her dad was cooking bacon and burning toast—the usual on a Sunday morning. Remembering the crazy dream she'd had the night before, she poked her head out from under the quilt—

—and saw Charlotte Brontë splashing what looked like pretty cold water on her face from a bowl that fit into a little hole cut in a wooden stand.

Carly's heart skipped a beat. So it wasn't a dream. Or at least, not a dream like any Carly'd had before. She poked the pillow by her head surreptitiously. It felt real enough.

"Good morning," said Carly brightly. And she meant it. Finally, after all her planning with Francesca, she was in the middle of an adventure. Who cared if she didn't know what sort, exactly? Having Francesca with her and knowing her family wasn't worried about her were the only things that could improve being back in—when *was* she back in time to? She'd have to ask. Or maybe there was a newspaper lying around.

Charlotte looked over.

"Good morning, Caroline," she said. "I've put out your cream wool dress, as today promises to be rather cold for the time of year. After you have washed and dressed, you may join us downstairs for breakfast."

With a brisk nod, she left the room. Carly wondered if the "us" Charlotte had mentioned included Branwell and felt a shiver of unease run up her spine. Determinedly, she shrugged it off. She wasn't going to let anyone, including Branwell, ruin her first real adventure. Sniffing defiantly, she got up to look at the dress Charlotte had laid out.

The cream-colored frock was so pretty—its full skirt swished satisfactorily just below her knees, and her half boots had darling buttons. Carly sighed happily. She'd always known it would be tremendous fun to dress like this. She only wished she were grown up enough to wear long dresses like the Brontë sisters, with full skirts and puffed sleeves—but she'd probably have to wear a corset, too, and she was dubious about how fun *that* would be.

The wool stockings were itchy, but not as bad as Carly had feared. Wool versus fleece was one of the things Carly and her dad argued about before camping trips: Carly said fleece was more comfy; George Keene always pointed out that wool was warm even when it was wet. Plus, he said, it was self-extinguishing—fleece would melt right onto your skin if you got too close to a camp fire, but wool wouldn't burn unless you kept it in the flames. Now, Carly thought, she wouldn't mind wearing wool if it was as pretty as this dress. The yoke even had a ribbon decoration that matched the hem.

With a start, Carly remembered Charlotte was waiting. She tied her hair back with a matching cream ribbon that Charlotte had left on top of the dress and ran lightly downstairs, admiring the way her skirt billowed as she moved.

The door to the dining room was open and Carly was relieved to see no sign of Branwell. Feeling pleased with the world, she paused in the doorway and did her best curtsey—a skill her Southern grandmother, the one who thought French camp was a good idea—had insisted she learn.

"Good morning Mr. Brontë, Miss Brontë, Miss Emily, Miss Anne."

The other occupants of the room looked up with varying expressions of surprise.

Mr. Brontë nodded vaguely in her direction and said, "Yes, yes, very well."

Charlotte merely nodded. Anne smiled. Emily glanced out the window, where grey clouds sat low and glowering, before sniffing and returning to her breakfast.

Somewhat dampened by this reception, Carly ate her burned toast, bacon, and porridge in silence—and used the time to study the various Brontës.

Mr. Brontë sat at the head of the table with Emily at his right and Anne at his left. Charlotte sat at the foot of the table; Carly was on her right, next to Anne. The seat beside Emily was empty. Carly wondered, a little wickedly, what might happen if she took someone else's seat without warning. At her house, her parents usually sat at either end of the table, but she and her brother switched sides all the time.

Watching Mr. Brontë, she realized he wasn't fully blind (neither Anne nor Emily had to help him eat his breakfast), but he did need to be told what dish was being handed to him.

As soon as Carly finished her tea and slightly lumpy porridge, Charlotte rose and said, "Caroline, let us begin your lessons."

"Okay, but can you tell me what year it is?"

Everyone in the room stared.

"Whatever do you mean?" asked Charlotte.

"Well, what year is it? Right now? I . . . I can't remember," said Carly, wishing she'd just looked for a newspaper.

"1846. Are you feeling well?" asked Charlotte.

"Oh, yeah, I'm fine," said Carly weakly. *1846!*

"Then stop using slang and come with me," Charlotte said.

Obediently, Carly followed Charlotte into the book-lined study where Tabby had found Carly the previous day. Carly couldn't help but stare at the chair in which she'd woken up. If she sat in it again, would she be whisked back home? Did she want to be whisked back home? She hadn't had a chance to explore yet, or enjoy being in a different time. This was her adventure, after all!

Carly resolved to sit only in the other chair near the empty fire grate, just in case.

"Let us begin with history," said Charlotte. "After I select the appropriate books, we will go up to the school room. Your mother informed me that you had reached the reign of Queen Elizabeth."

How odd, thought Carly. *My mother doesn't seem to know much about Queen Elizabeth whenever I bring up the Spanish Armada. Oh. Not my mother—Caroline's mother.*

The thought made Carly feel so much like an imposter that she was sure Charlotte would notice. But somehow, Charlotte didn't.

History as Charlotte taught it was nothing like history in Carly's Alaskan school. Carly found the repetition of dates tedious and was dismayed to learn that Charlotte expected her to memorize an entire list, along with a short description of each event. She could do it, but it would be boring.

"Wouldn't it be more interesting if we read Queen Elizabeth the First's speech to the troops when she thought the Spanish Armada was coming?" said Carly. "My dad and I read it together. The best part is when she says she 'has the heart and stomach of a king.'"

"There is only one Queen Elizabeth, Caroline. And the methods by which I teach are those calculated to best help you learn your lessons," said Charlotte. "But if you continue to display such quickness of mind, we may eventually advance beyond the normal curriculum."

After looking outside at the sky, Charlotte decided the weather had improved enough to allow for an art lesson, so the two repaired to the garden, armed with sketchpads and charcoal. Carly enjoyed drawing, so the time passed quickly. She tried to follow Charlotte's instructions for how to properly render the neglected flower border they were sketching, though it would have been fun if more flowers were blooming—really, how many scraggly bushes could one draw?

Still, it was nice to be outside. To take her mind off the fact that the tree on the left side of her sketch looked like it had been struck by lightning and burned for a solid week, Carly brought up the book of poetry Charlotte had mentioned the day before.

"Miss Brontë, may I see a copy of your book of poems? The piece you quoted yesterday was so lovely."

Charlotte looked over at Carly's drawing and said, "The birch tree on the left appears to have suffered an unhappy accident."

Carly waited to see if she'd say anything else.

Charlotte looked over at the actual birch tree, which was in the best of health.

"Very well, I will lend you my copy after tea. Now, try to correctly capture the bowed arc of the elm. It is the result of years of battering winds."

The rest of the morning sped by so fast that Carly was surprised when Charlotte told her it was time to return indoors for lunch. It was liver with onions and turnips; she didn't eat much. After lunch came her first French lesson, which went even more dreadfully than Carly had feared. It was more memorization and repetition: "*Je suis, tu es, il/elle est, nous sommes, vous êtes, ils/elles sont*," and Carly struggled to remember which "s" sounds were silent and which vocalized and which "l" sounds were an "l" and which sounded like a "y."

"Caroline, your pronunciation is dreadful," said Charlotte, and Carly felt the familiar surge of shame that she couldn't do this as easily as she did the rest of her schoolwork. "But perhaps if instead of merely repeating after me you also look at each word as we go, you might find it easier," finished Charlotte, handing the grammar and vocabulary book to Carly.

"If I can't picture the word, I can't remember it or even say it," Carly admitted.

"Then let us try this method," said Charlotte, smiling gently at Carly and beginning again. "*Je suis . . .*"

Carly took a deep breath and summoned all her concentration.

Finally, lessons were finished for the day, and Charlotte left Carly alone with the promised slender volume. The book was titled simply, *Poems*, and was by Currer, Ellis, and Acton Bell. Obviously the Brontë sisters had kept their initials but given themselves new names, Carly thought. What made less sense to her was *why*. Perhaps women weren't supposed to be writing poetry?

Carly started reading and was amazed at how melancholy most of the poems were. She liked them, but they weren't very *fun*. She was so distracted that when she saw Branwell at dinner, she hardly remembered his odd behavior from the night before, and the meal passed uneventfully.

Immediately afterwards, she turned to Charlotte.

"Miss Brontë, can I go upstairs and read in bed for a bit?"

"'May' I go upstairs, Caroline. Very well, but please be careful with the candle," said Charlotte.

Upstairs, Carly snuggled into bed to escape the chill. Before she returned to the book of poems, she spent a moment wiggling her toes against the hot brick Charlotte had sent up to warm the bed for her. How terribly romantic it was to be reading poetry by candlelight in an old stone house!

Despite missing her family and Francesca, and despite Charlotte's horror at her appalling French accent and constant grammar errors, Carly would not have traded her chance to be part of a real, live adventure for anything.

The wind had been quiet all day, but Carly's eye was drawn to the title of a poem, and she eagerly flipped to the page:

> *Lines Composed in a Wood on a Windy Day*
> *MY soul is awakened, my spirit is soaring*
> *And carried aloft on the wings of the breeze;*
> *For above and around me the wild wind is roaring,*
> *Arousing to rapture the earth and the seas.*
>
> *The long withered grass in the sunshine is glancing,*
> *The bare trees are tossing their branches on high;*
> *The dead leaves, beneath them, are merrily dancing,*
> *The white clouds are scudding across the blue sky.*
>
> *I wish I could see how the ocean is lashing*
> *The foam of its billows to whirlwinds of spray;*
> *I wish I could see how its proud waves are dashing,*
> *And hear the wild roar of their thunder today!*

Carly wanted to run outside and see this for herself—*the wild wind roaring*! It was so exciting, the way it was written about in the poem. Perhaps tomorrow she could convince Charlotte to take her for a walk to see some of the countryside. It wouldn't be neglecting her studies, Carly reasoned. It would be adding to them by teaching her some natural history. She'd never been to England, much less Yorkshire, and she very much wanted to see the moors. She supposed she couldn't use the fact that she was from Alaska as a good reason to walk about the countryside—what would poor Anne think of Alaska when the thought of Carly's, or Caroline's, parents in India worried her so?

With a giggle, Carly skipped the next poem (the title, *Stanzas*, sounded boring), and started to read the following one.

Almost immediately, she said, "Emily must have written this—I can't imagine Charlotte or Anne saying something like:

> *"Cruel Death ! The young leaves droop and languish;*
> *Evening's gentle air may still restore–*
> *No ! the morning sunshine mocks my anguish–*
> *Time, for me, must never blossom more !*
>
> *"Strike it down, that other boughs may flourish*
> *Where that perished sapling used to be;*
> *Thus, at least, its mouldering corpse will nourish*
> *That from which it sprung–Eternity."*

Carly read it aloud with great feeling, lingering mournfully on the words "mouldering corpse." *Awesome; no wimpy happy sunshine poems for Emily!* thought Carly.

But as she was about to give another giggle and find a poem more to her taste, the wind started to blow and something gave a sharp tap-tap against the glass of the window. Carly gasped and held up her candle to see better, but the shutters revealed nothing.

"I'm sure it's a tree branch or a climbing rose or something," she whispered.

Another sharp tap at the window made her pull back. A floorboard creaked as though someone had stepped on it.

"I *ought* to stop being silly, get out of bed, and go see what that noise is. But I don't dare. And the floor is cold." Carly thought this sounded like a weak excuse, even to her own ears, but she still couldn't make herself move. A cold fear crept over her, and she felt like she couldn't breathe right.

"It's the wind. It has to be," she said, putting one hand to her throat in an unconscious gesture. The hand holding the candle trembled, and the shadows danced on the wall. Carly hastily put the taper on the bedside table.

"I'm going to sleep now. There's nothing there but the wind." Carly looked over at the candle. She ought to blow it out, but the thought of listening in darkness to the wind tap-tapping and the floorboards creaking was too much for her.

"I'll let it burn until Charlotte comes up. I wouldn't want her to stumble around in the dark, anyway," she said.

With one last, long look at the tightly shuttered window, Carly curled up under the covers, thinking to herself that this house was much less friendly at night than it was during the day.

↭

The next morning, she again awoke to find Charlotte laying out her clothes. Carly immediately looked at the window—nothing but sky. She walked over and peered out, craning her neck to see if there was anything near enough to have made the sounds she'd heard last night. But there was nothing. No tree stood near enough to reach the window, and there were no climbing flowers against the side of the house. Carly shivered.

When she came down to breakfast (more speedily today, because the navy blue serge dress she was wearing wasn't so pretty as the cream wool), she ventured to ask Charlotte about the mysterious sounds.

"Miss Brontë, did you hear anything last night when you came up? Before I fell asleep, I was sure there was something tapping against the window, but I don't see how any of the tree branches could have reached it."

"I heard nothing out of the ordinary. Perhaps you imagined it. Newcomers to the moors often find the sounds of the wind unsettling."

Carly had no trouble believing *that*, but she was also sure that it hadn't been the wind last night. She stirred her porridge gloomily—lumpy again, and not even any bacon to make up for it.

Emily looked up from her tea.

"Perhaps it was a restless soul from the graveyard."

"What graveyard?" Carly asked.

"The one on the other side of the house, opposite the garden. This is a parsonage," said Emily condescendingly. "The rector needs to be near the church and therefore . . . " she paused and added with relish, "the graveyard."

"Really, Emily, you make it sound dreadful. I'm sure that no one Father has laid to rest is wandering about haunting us! Or anyone buried by the new curate, Mr. Nicholls, now that he is here to help with Father's duties," said Anne, looking shocked.

"Mr. Nicholls is very gentlemanly. I'm sure no one is haunting our bedroom window because of *him*," said Charlotte.

Carly regretted bringing the subject up in front of Emily, and was glad she hadn't mentioned the creaking floorboards. A change in topic would be good, she thought.

"Could we take a walk on the moors today? I would like to see them!" Carly saw the curious glances from the three sisters and hastily added: "More closely, that is. They look so beautiful."

"If the weather is fine, I would say that I could take you after your morning lessons, but I must make up some charity baskets to bring to the village tomorrow as part of Father's ministry, so I cannot spare the time," said Charlotte.

"I could take her, as long as the walk was not too far," said Anne.

Carly looked gratefully at her.

"Anne, you must be careful of your health. You are not strong after your last indisposition." Charlotte chided her gently.

"I will dress warmly, and a little walk will do me good, I'm sure of it," said Anne. "We won't go very far."

Charlotte considered the matter for a moment.

"Very well, but you must both promise to be careful and not do anything rash."

"Of course we won't," said Anne.

Carly bounced in her seat, excited. She was going to see the moors! All she had to do was survive her morning lesson in geography. No doubt it would be as dull as history yesterday— Charlotte had said something daunting about putting together a segmented map, and Carly had no idea what the borders of countries looked like in 1846. She hoped Alaska would be there, even if it still belonged to Russia.

But then! Then she would be free to go outside and explore. She hadn't realized how tired she was of sitting all the time: sitting inside to study, sitting in the garden to draw, sitting on the piano bench to practice . . .

Now maybe *her* spirit could be "carried aloft on the wings of the breeze."

CHAPTER FIVE

Carly sat impatiently through her morning lesson. The segmented map was of the counties in England, which Carly had never seen before. However, years of helping her grandfather with puzzles let her piece it together quickly even though she relied on trial and error. At least Carly knew Hertfordshire was not near Derbyshire, because whenever her grandmother visited, they watched *Pride and Prejudice*.

"And," Carly said to Charlotte, "Mr. Darcy thinks Lizzie might not want to live *too* near her family."

"You have read Miss Austen's novel?" asked Charlotte, raising her eyebrows.

"Oh, no, not yet. But I've seen the movie and my grandmother says Jane Austen is hilarious," said Carly, forgetting for a moment that movies did not yet exist.

"Seen the what?" exclaimed Charlotte.

"The . . . I forget?" said Carly, and added quickly, "Do you like *Pride and Prejudice?*"

Charlotte sniffed. "I have not read it, for from everything I hear, Miss Austen lacks passion in her characters. But *she* is still much admired."

The acerbic note in Charlotte's voice was impossible to miss.

"You will oblige me, Caroline, by studying the counties until you can tell me not only *where* they are, but the names of their principal cities. Let us now turn to a review of the history you learned yesterday."

Carly almost groaned aloud. She had a good memory but wasn't used to memorizing so many things at once and so stumbled through the second half of the examination. Charlotte sighed.

"I think you should stay inside and apply yourself to your history instead of going for a walk, Caroline. Sir Francis Drake circumnavigated the globe between 1577 and 1580. He was not sailing in 1565."

"Oh, no! *Please* don't make me stay inside!" cried Carly, bitter disappointment welling up within her. "I want to go outside to explore. I haven't seen *anything* yet."

Charlotte frowned.

"You must attend properly to your studies, Caroline. You are bright, but you must apply yourself all the more for that. It would be a shame to waste your talents through laziness as so many girls do."

"I won't! I promise. But you said I could go, and I hate sitting around all the time. It's the *worst*. Don't you find it boring too?"

Charlotte hesitated, and then her lips thinned.

"It does not matter whether I think sitting inside and teaching is boring. With my father's eyesight so poor and Branwell . . ." she trailed off, squared her shoulders, and continued. "My duty is plain. Emily has had to oversee the running of the household since the death of our Aunt Branwell, and I must attend to the business of the parish and to your education. We all, my sisters and I, must work, no matter how little we wish it," she finished in an almost gentle tone.

It was Carly's turn to frown. Were Charlotte and her sisters *that* trapped by their duties?

"Of course, everyone has to work, but it isn't fair that you don't also get to do some things for yourself. Everyone deserves time off to do stuff they like."

Charlotte gave a laugh, the first Carly had heard from her.

"And the 'stuff' you like is going for walks outside?" she said.

Carly smiled. "And reading in bed."

"Well, if you give me your assurances that you will be diligent in your studying this afternoon and stop using unladylike words such as 'stuff,' then you may go with Anne for a *short* walk on the moors."

"Oh, thank you!" said Carly, bouncing in her seat. "I'll work extra hard this afternoon, I promise!"

"See that you do. Now, go fetch your coat and bonnet."

Carly sighed happily as she went to get her coat. Finally, she was getting outside! And she would get to wear a bonnet, something she'd always wanted to do. Carly was sure that her hair would curl charmingly from under the brim, which would frame her face in a most delightful manner. That's what always happened to heroines like Sarah Crewe or Meg March in the books Carly's grandmother gave her.

In the books Carly's mother gave her, on the other hand, heroines like Caddie Woodlawn or Laura Ingalls were always losing their bonnets or having the ribbons come off or forgetting to wear them and getting freckled. The bridge of Carly's nose already had a few freckles and she burned easily, so she figured she'd better hope the bonnet charmingly framed her face.

Anne interrupted these musings by saying, with a slight smile,

"Shall we venture out, Caroline?"

"Yes, please!" said Carly.

The air outside was brisk but not cold, and the sky was overcast but still bright. Despite her delicate looks, and Charlotte's obvious concerns about her health, Anne set a fast pace through the garden and the stand of trees behind it. Carly was pleased; she'd been worried they would just meander and get nowhere.

The trees stretched all the way along the back of the garden and house, offering some protection from the strong winds off the moor. It wasn't spring, or even really summer any more, but Carly still hoped some of the beauty of the heather and broom Anne had described would be visible.

The little path through the firs led her and Anne right to the edge of the moor. Majestic fells rolled away from them, eventually climbing up to high hills so distant they seemed covered in a purple haze.

Carly gasped in delight. She hadn't expected the moors to be so wild and beautiful. Most places felt tame to Carly after growing up in Alaska, but the moor reminded her of the interior of her home state—a vast space that seemed more open because there wasn't anything to distract the eye or block the view.

Thinking about Alaska sent a sudden rush of homesickness coursing through Carly. It surprised her and left her breathless. To distract herself, Carly stared at the scenery as hard as she could. She saw a few small cottages scattered in the distance off to her right. Beside her, Anne led the way along a well-worn track.

Each step further out onto the moors made it easier for Carly to push the upset away. She felt like the adventure was truly beginning. The air was fresh and scented by heather and broom; the breeze whisked around them, and she couldn't help running a few steps in sheer exuberance.

"It's so beautiful!" she said.

Anne laughed a soft laugh—the kind you use when you know if you laugh too hard, you will start to cough.

"We think so, but some people hate it."

"Why?" asked Carly. The moor seemed so interesting—the broom was tall and you could have lots of fun sneaking around in it, while the heather looked like a comfy place to lie out on a sunny day and watch birds or read.

"They think it bleak and unfriendly," said Anne.

"I think it's the kind of place that inspires poetry," said Carly, giving Anne a sly look.

"Yes, it has certainly inspired some of ours," Anne said.

Carly looked eagerly ahead to where the ground rose. A small hill hid what was immediately beyond. There was so much to explore; she wanted to run just to get a head start on everything there was to see and discover. Anne walked sedately along the path, while Carly ran first this way and then that, enjoying the freedom of being outside, of breathing fresh air, of seeing an entirely new place.

"Tickety-boooooo!" she shouted, hoping that somehow, back in Juneau, Francesca would hear her and know everything was well.

She ran ahead of Anne up over the crest of the hill and paused to look at a couple of songbirds flitting over the heather. Away to her left, she saw the white dots of sheep grazing on a hillside. When Anne caught up, Carly smiled at her.

"Why do you guys ever go indoors? This is so much better."

"I am glad you like it—to us it is the dearest place in the world. But do not be deceived: The wind is gentle today, but the weather here can turn quickly and be quite dangerous," said Anne.

Despite her glee at finally being outside, it was Carly who suggested turning toward home. She noticed that Anne's breath was coming more shortly and that she had coughed several times.

"You are right, Caroline. My sisters would never forgive me if I overexerted myself and fell ill again," Anne said.

Reluctantly, they walked back. Carly fell behind as they neared the belt of trees protecting the parsonage from the strong winds off the moors. She took as many deep breaths as she could, storing up the scent of fresh air and the feel of the breeze tugging wisps of hair out from under her bonnet. Pausing at the edge of the trees, Carly untied her bonnet and let it hang by its ribbon at her side while she took a last look at the moors.

As she turned to follow Anne, she felt the same sense of being watched that had haunted her on the island. Her stomach knotted in worry. Carly looked all around, squinting at the trees and foliage. Nothing. Hoping to escape it, she hurried inside and sat quietly through lunch, feeling miserably alone. If only Francesca were there to tell her that it would be okay, or that she was totally nuts. Either would make Carly feel better.

But she was alone. Carly shivered, thinking that the watchful silence had followed her from Alaska to Yorkshire—and from 2013 to 1846! Charlotte noticed her shiver and sent her to get a woolen shawl from their bedroom—though Carly swore she wasn't cold. As she came back down the stairs, trailing the shawl carelessly behind her, she heard raised voices.

Charlotte said something she couldn't quite hear, and then Branwell cut in,

"My head aches abominably! I must have some laudanum for it."

"You take entirely too much of the stuff," said Charlotte.

Carly crept a stair closer, listening.

"You have no idea what I suffer," said Branwell in a querulous tone.

"Oh, let him take it—he has already ruined the school for us. He may as well go to the devil in his own fashion," said Emily sharply.

Carly froze on the bottom step. *What school?* she wondered. *And what's laudanum?* Branwell sounded angry and pleading; Emily sounded bitter; and Charlotte was upset. Carly knew from watching the siblings that they were a close family—how had Branwell ruined things for his sisters?

Realizing she would soon be missed, Carly ran quietly back up three stairs and made sure to walk loudly as she came down again. When she reentered the dining room, she saw Branwell sitting with his head in his hands. Emily watched Charlotte with pursed lips and tightly folded arms as Charlotte brought forward a small bottle and put a few drops from it in Branwell's glass. He gulped it down and left the room without another word. Anne sighed.

"It is a pity laudanum is so expensive," she said.

"The pity is that he can't control himself," snapped Emily.

Carly decided it was the wrong moment to ask what laudanum was. An awkward silence stretched, which Charlotte broke by saying,

"Come along, Caroline. Let us see if you are any more proficient at learning the German tongue than the French."

It was going to be a long afternoon. Carly didn't see how she could possibly concentrate on German when all she wanted to do was talk to Francesca about what was happening and make sure she wasn't going crazy. But her thoughts got her no closer to solving the mystery—though her abstraction did earn her a reprimand from Charlotte.

"Caroline, you promised me more application to your studies if I allowed you to go for a walk. I do not find this satisfactory."

"I'm sorry. I was thinking about something else," said Carly.

"Obviously," said Charlotte. "Please turn your attention to page two of the German grammar and repeat each of the words after me. *Der Junge*, the boy."

"*Der Junge*," said Carly, trying to focus.

"*Die Jungen*, the boys."

To her surprise, once she started paying attention, German was easier than French—at least the letters sounded the way they were written.

"Hmm," said Charlotte. "Let us see if you become more proficient if you write the words out. Start with the German, then next to each write its English translation. Then we shall erase the German and you will see how many you can remember. Then the same for the English," said Charlotte, fetching a slate.

Normally Carly would have found this tedious beyond words, but the novelty of getting to use a slate like Anne Shirley combined with the peaceful monotony of writing the vocabulary was soothing to her disturbed spirits, and she worked steadily.

"You are not as naturally adept at foreign languages as the other subjects, but your hard work will help you overcome that deficiency," said Charlotte eventually.

"Thanks . . . I think," said Carly, happy that Charlotte recognized how hard she was working to forge through the impenetrable thicket of foreign languages.

After the German lesson was over, Charlotte left Carly to practice the piano alone while she checked on her father and finished putting together the charity baskets. Just before Charlotte left, Carly felt bold enough to ask what laudanum was. Charlotte looked at her, surprised.

"But surely you know! It is a draught used to relieve pain and help an ill person sleep."

"So it's a drug?" asked Carly.

"Yes," said Charlotte shortly.

"Is your brother sick?" Carly asked, thinking an illness might explain Branwell's odd behavior on the stairs.

"Not with anything catching," said Charlotte, rubbing her temples.

"Oh, is he depressed like Francesca's dad? Mr. Erikson felt a lot better after he started taking medicine," said Carly. "But he can't drink while he takes it—maybe Branwell shouldn't drink so much wine."

"Whether he suffers from melancholia or not, and how much wine he drinks, are not proper topics for a young girl—nor are they any of your concern," snapped Charlotte. "Now practice the pianoforte while I attend to other business, Caroline."

And with that she left.

Carly thought over everything she'd learned. First, Branwell drank a lot; second, he took a drug for pain but wasn't sick with anything catching; third, he had somehow ruined a school for his sisters (the first and second were enough for Carly to see how that might be possible).

Fourth, there was a Silent Watchfulness both here and at home in Juneau.

Carly sat, hands resting on the keys. She might be getting to wear pretty old-fashioned dresses and learn to pour tea, but something was wrong here. Carly began to imagine cold, ghostly whispers haunting her forever—to suit the mood, she started playing "The Music of the Night" from *The Phantom of the Opera*. But she kept pausing to look over her shoulder, just in case. It did not improve her performance.

When she was thinking that she couldn't stand being alone any longer in the room, with its creeping shadows and chilly air, Anne entered to tell her dinner was ready. Carly practically leapt off the piano bench with relief.

"Whatever were you playing? It sounded most outlandish," said Anne.

"Something that mirrors the creepy atmosphere," said Carly with a shiver.

Anne raised her eyebrows. "I promise you there is nothing to fear from the moors."

"It's not the moors that scare me," said Carly, with perfect truthfulness.

"Whatever it is, don't let your romantic imagination run away with you," said Anne with a smile.

Carly didn't think it was her imagination, but Anne's calm cheerfulness made her feel less on edge.

When they joined the family for dinner, Charlotte was too busy talking to her father about parish business—what duties he could continue, which he ought to turn over to the new curate, Mr. Nicholls—to spare Carly more than a brief reprimand for her odd choice in music. Carly felt too happy after Anne's calming dismissal of her fears to much care, and applied herself to her dinner with enthusiasm—though the meat on her plate appeared to be mutton, and she quickly learned that rutabagas were not her favorite vegetable.

After she had gotten into bed, Carly wondered anew why her adventure had brought her to the Brontës. She needed more information than an unpredictable feeling of being watched could give her; how was she supposed to figure anything out if the only things she was learning were German nouns and English counties?

Carly sat up sharply in bed. A-ha! She'd sneak downstairs and eavesdrop. She wished she had some of Fred and George Weasley's Extendable Ears so she could hide upstairs, but she'd have to do it the old-fashioned way: quietly.

The stairway was dim and steep, and Carly moved with caution. *I do an awful lot of hanging out at the bottom of this staircase*, she thought—and then she heard Emily's voice.

"I think his name shall be Heathcliff."

"Heathcliff?" Anne's voice.

"Yes," said Emily. "I despise all the conventional names for men, and Heathcliff will be anything but a weak excuse for a man."

"If it suits his character, then it is well chosen," came Charlotte's voice.

"That was very disobedient of you, to go wandering around the house at night."

After Charlotte left the room, Carly let out a big breath. She might be in trouble, but she'd learned some interesting things. Not at all chastened by Charlotte's reprimand, she opened the book of poems and read until her eyes grew heavy.

Her favorite poem from that night started out:

> *How brightly glistening in the sun*
> *The woodland ivy plays!*
> *While yonder beeches from their barks*
> *Reflect his silver rays.*

She sleepily repeated the lines a few times before putting the book away and blowing out her candle.

Almost immediately she heard it. Tap-tap-tap at the window.

Carly didn't move. Maybe it would go away. Tap-tap-tap, and a low sigh. With that sound, Carly's fear turned to anger. This was ridiculous. It was just the wind in the trees. She would prove it! Carly jumped out of bed and ran over to the window.

"There!" she cried, throwing open the shutters defiantly.

The thin, pale face of a girl stared back at her. The girl's hair was long and straight and still—even though Carly could hear the wild wind through the glass.

Carly gave a choked cry of horror and tried to slam the shutters. They wouldn't move. The girl raised a claw-like hand and pointed at Carly. Even through the glass Carly could hear her words:

"Save my sisters or you will not save yourself."

Carly let go of the shutters and blindly struggled toward the door in the dark. She had to get Charlotte. She'd be safe if she could just get to the others.

Her groping hands found the door latch. A glance back into the room showed nothing at the window, but it was too dark to be certain.

Scrambling down the stairs as fast as she could on legs that seemed to have turned to lead, Carly burst into the dining room, where the Brontës had resumed their walking and scribbling.

"Caroline!" exclaimed Charlotte wrathfully.

Carly stopped. "I saw a . . ." she was gasping from fright. "I saw a . . . a *ghost!*"

There was a short pause.

"Is she mad, or lying?" asked Emily, looking at Charlotte.

"No! No, I'm not," said Carly, trying to hold back tears of fright.

"You had a nightmare," said Anne in a soothing tone.

"No, please!" cried Carly again, dashing a tear away from her cheek and staring at the three women, her heart still pounding in her chest. They would not believe her without proof. She wrapped her arms tightly around herself. Her fright was mixed with the loneliness she had felt before. There was no one but herself to understand.

"Come along, I shall walk you upstairs so you can see that there is nothing of which you should be afraid," said Charlotte.

She took Carly by the arm, more gently this time, and led her back upstairs. Charlotte held her candle up high and circled it slowly about the room.

But there were no ghosts to be found.

☙ CHAPTER SIX ☙

Carly awoke, her eyes heavy; she had lain awake for hours the night before, too frightened to sleep. It was not that she objected to ghosts as part of her adventure, but she didn't like *angry* ghosts who threatened her. What had she ever done to a ghost from 1846?

But Charlotte gave her no time to ponder the events of the night before. Instead, she hurried Carly through dressing and breakfast. She would not let Carly wear her cream wool, insisting instead on the serviceable blue serge (Carly reflected bitterly that "serviceable" always meant "not pretty").

Immediately after breakfast, the pair put on their coats and bonnets and Carly picked up three of the baskets Charlotte had prepared for the poor.

"Remember, there is broth in the baskets, so hold them steady," said Charlotte, picking up the other four.

"Just like in *Little Women*!" Carly said without thinking.

"Hmmm?" said Charlotte, busy rearranging her baskets.

"*Little Women*—the March sisters take baskets . . ." Carly trailed off. She didn't know when Louisa May Alcott had written *Little Women*. In her copy, the pictures showed the sisters wearing dresses much like the ones she and the Brontës wore, but still, better to be cautious.

"Never mind, it's just a book I read once." She hefted her baskets. "Let's get this show on the road."

"Caroline, at times your speech shows a lowness and vulgarity for which I simply cannot account. Where do you learn such phrases?" asked Charlotte.

Carly thought fast.

"The stable boy," she said. Stable boys always used lots of slang in books.

"I didn't know your parents kept horses. What have they done with them while the house is shut up in their absence?"

Before Carly could come up with an answer, Charlotte continued.

"However that may be, you will refrain from repeating such vulgar phrases. It is not ladylike."

"Yes, Miss Brontë," said Carly, happy she hadn't had to explain where her imaginary parents kept their imaginary horses while they sailed to India.

"And you may call me Miss Charlotte—Miss Brontë is too formal, now that you are living with us."

"Yes, Miss Charlotte," said Carly.

As they left the house, Carly had her first view of the graveyard. It was tucked in close to the left side of the parsonage, and she thought uncomfortably that it wouldn't be difficult for a ghost to wander over from the graveyard to her window. Then she scolded herself for thinking foolish things. *It's stupid to get the heebie-jeebies in broad daylight!*

The walk to the village of Haworth from the parsonage was short, but the baskets were heavy, and Carly and Charlotte rested several times on the grassy verge by the side of the road. Hedges shut off the view into any of the fields they passed.

As they walked, Charlotte gave Carly instructions on what to expect.

"You are not to go into any of the houses with me, and do not touch my dress after I've visited the Martins—I hear young Bridget Martin has typhoid. The others are infirm, poor, or sick with something less infectious like consumption. You still mustn't come in, though—I'd never forgive myself if you took ill."

"Don't go into the houses; don't touch you after you visit the Martins," repeated Carly. "What else besides broth is in the baskets?" she asked Charlotte, puffing as she set hers down to rest.

"Restorative calf's foot jelly that Emily made, woolen socks for some, the clear broth, and a few vegetables," said Charlotte, also resting.

When they reached the village Carly looked around with interest. It was dirtier than she expected, despite the thatched roofs on the houses and vegetables growing in the yards. Most of the villagers were not dressed as well as she and Charlotte, and did not look particularly healthy.

Charlotte led her down the main street and into a small side lane. Carly was *not* ready for the trench that ran in front of the houses. She had to cross a little footbridge over it to reach the lane where Charlotte waited in front of some of the poorer houses.

"What is that?" Carly asked, nearly gagging from the smell.

"What is what?" asked Charlotte, looking around.

"That!" said Carly, pointing at the ditch.

"Oh, the sewer, of course."

"The *sewer*? But it's just . . . sitting here, right in the open!" said Carly in horror.

"I know. We have petitioned the village council to fill it in an attempt to improve health conditions, but no one likes to bear the expense," said Charlotte with a sigh. "Upwards of a dozen families use each privy."

"That is so gross," said Carly. "No wonder there are so many sick people!"

Charlotte raised an eyebrow at Carly's usage of "gross," but continued to speak without reprimanding her. "It also concerns my father that the village well water comes from the hill upon which the parsonage sits."

"Why is that a problem?" asked Carly.

"We believe the graveyard does not contribute to the quality of the water," said Charlotte.

"What?" said Carly, horrified. "People are drinking *grave* water?!"

"I would not put it just like that. But it would be better to have a new well dug."

At the first few houses they visited, Carly sat patiently outside with the baskets and listened through the open doors to Charlotte's conversations. Mostly they were about the health of whomever they were visiting, the weather, and the price of wool.

"Why is everyone so interested in the price of wool?" she asked after she heard it mentioned for the third time.

"Most people here make their living from sheep—raising them, spinning, and then working in the textile factories along the river weaving the wool."

The Martins' house was the last stop. The minute she saw it, Carly could tell something was wrong. All the curtains were drawn, even though it was mid-morning. A tall young man with impressive side-whiskers came out and stood in the door-way. Carly noticed as she looked more closely that he wore a white collar above his black coat—he was a priest. He passed a hand over his face.

"Mr. Nicholls," said Charlotte, setting down her empty baskets by Carly and taking the remaining full one forward.

"Miss Brontë," said the young man, looking up and bow-ing.

"What are you doing here?" asked Charlotte.

"I'm sorry to say that my services were needed. Young Bridget Martin has passed away."

Carly gasped. Charlotte and Mr. Nicholls looked over at her, Mr. Nicholls as though he was noticing her for the first time, and Charlotte with an expression of pity on her face.

"Died?" said Carly. "How old was she?"

"Five or six, I believe," said Mr. Nicholls.

"Five," said Charlotte sadly. "How terrible for Mr. and Mrs. Martin after losing Jimmy last year."

"More than one of their kids has died?" asked Carly in hor-ror.

"Caroline, sit over there and compose yourself," said Char-lotte. "I must take this basket in, and I don't wish you to be too close."

Carly sat, her eyes filled with tears. Five! Francesca's littlest sister Madeline was five. James was six. Another wave of homesickness filled her. She wanted to see James, to make sure he and her parents were all right. But how could she get back to her family?

The image of Charlotte and Mr. Nicholls' faces as they discussed little Bridget Martin wouldn't leave her mind. They had been sad, yes, but even worse, they hadn't seemed surprised that a little girl had *died*. In fact, Carly realized, they had been expecting it.

Carly felt sick. Why didn't Charlotte *do* something? Where was the doctor? A village this size must have a doctor. Maybe I should go find him, Carly thought in a rush. She stood up blindly, not sure where to go.

A pair of women from the village walked by, and what they said made Carly sit back down.

"Tsk, the curtains all drawn. The poor Martins, to lose another one. Mr. Martin thought the world of Bridget."

"Look, that must be the young lady to whom Miss Brontë is governess. I hear her parents went off to India."

"A heathen place. I don't hold with foreign parts myself."

"Very proper, Miss Lynch, I'm sure. What is Miss Brontë thinking, bringing the girl near a house with typhoid? I wouldn't let my May near it for anything."

"Indeed Mrs. Smythe, indeed. Such a pity about the brother—ruining their reputations with his drinking and *other* excesses. But I suppose people who go gallivanting to India can't be too choosy about who looks after their children."

The two women were almost out of earshot when Charlotte came out of the house. Almost, but not quite. Looking at her face, Carly could tell Charlotte heard the last sentence:

"That brother of theirs ruined their school, and he'll ruin more than that before he's through, mark my words."

Charlotte stiffened, but remained silent.

Mr. Nicholls also came out of the house and shut the door behind him.

"We must go," said Charlotte. "There is no more we can do for the Martins today."

"May I escort you both back towards the parsonage? My path lies with yours for much of the way," said Mr. Nicholls.

"Thank you, Mr. Nicholls, you may," said Charlotte. "Come along, Caroline, but don't come too close until I have had time to change my dress."

So Carly walked slowly behind Mr. Nicholls and Charlotte. The two grown-ups discussed the funeral arrangements and other members of the parish who might need aid. Carly did not listen closely. She was too shocked by the death of Bridget Martin and the words of the gossipy women.

Near the parsonage, Mr. Nicholls left them, telling Charlotte he would call on Mr. Brontë in the morning to discuss a leak in the bell tower. He pressed Charlotte's hand briefly and walked off down the lane.

Inside, Charlotte and Carly found the whole house in a subdued uproar. Charlotte went immediately upstairs to change, leaving Carly in the front hallway to stack the now empty baskets. Emily appeared from the direction of the kitchen, wearing an apron over her dress.

"Where is my sister?" she demanded.

"She went upstairs to change. Bridget Martin died of typhoid. Why?" asked Carly.

"Don't ask impertinent questions," said Emily, going upstairs without bothering to take off the apron. As soon as she vanished into Charlotte and Carly's room, Anne came out of Mr. Brontë's study.

Carly heard Mr. Brontë saying, "Has she returned? Anne, bring her here immediately."

Anne looked at Carly.

"Where is my sister?"

"Upstairs with Emily. Why?"

Again Carly got no answer. Anne had already started up the stairs.

Carly looked around, half expecting Branwell to appear and demand to know where Charlotte was as well. For a moment it was still, and then the three sisters came out of the bedroom, talking in hushed voices. Carly tried to look unobtrusive so they wouldn't think to send her away.

"The letter is from Brussels," Anne was saying.

"I heard you the first three times," said Charlotte.

"Father has not opened it, for it is addressed to you, but he demands you read it aloud to him," said Emily.

"Oh!" exclaimed Charlotte in a stricken tone. "Am I to have no privacy, no things that may be kept silent?"

"How dare he write? How dare he!" said Emily. "With no thought as to what this might mean to you! If I were a man, I should go to Brussels and give him a good beating for his imprudence!"

"No, oh, no!" said Charlotte, holding onto the banister for support.

"Perhaps it is not from *him*," said Anne.

"Who, who else could it be?" said Charlotte, the hand on the banister going to her throat.

"What if it is *Madame* Heger who writes?" asked Anne in a low voice. With that thought, which appeared to horrify her sisters more than any previous, the three reached the bottom of the stairs and noticed Carly still standing by the front door.

Charlotte made a visible effort to collect herself.

"Caroline, there is some urgent business I must see to. Go and practice the piano for half an hour. Then work on your French verbs."

With that, the sisters swept into Mr. Brontë's study and shut the door. Carly stood for a minute longer in the hall, in case anything else interesting was going to happen, but the door remained closed.

Upstairs, Carly went dutifully to the piano, but before she could pick out a piece, the door banged open and Branwell strode in. His red hair stood on end and his neck cloth was in disarray, as though he had been tugging at it. He didn't appear to notice Carly, but instead rooted in a cupboard in the corner of the room, muttering to himself.

"Where is it? I know I hid it somewhere! How dare he write back? Emily knows that man isn't half as clever and charming as he thinks he is, even if he did call her a genius. But how to make Charlotte see? I can't *think* in this stuffy house! Where is it? Ah!"

With this exclamation, Carly saw him pull a bottle out of the cupboard. Branwell hurried from the room without once looking at the piano bench where Carly sat, frozen.

What in heaven's name was happening? Carly knew from conversation around the dining room table that Charlotte had recently returned from Brussels in Belgium, where she and Emily had studied French and taught literature and music. Emily always ended discussions of their time abroad by saying dramatically, "I could never be parted from my beloved moors again—I'd rather starve!"

Charlotte never said she missed Brussels, but the subject seemed to depress her.

Carly idly played scales, her fingers moving up and down the keys while she thought. There was something the matter with Charlotte—and not just the worry all three sisters felt about Branwell and his drinking and laudanum use. When grown-ups didn't want to let kids see what was wrong, Carly thought, it usually meant the trouble lay with their hearts.

She mulled this over. Had Charlotte been showing signs of heartache? Would Carly know what those signs looked like if she saw them? Maybe not. This is why it would have been useful to have an older sister or brother, Carly thought. Then she could have observed what being in love looked like first-hand. As it was, Carly was used to people who said what they meant. Whereas everyone here seemed to speak about their feelings in code. It was very vexing.

And what about the letter that had just arrived? Did that give her any clues? It was from Brussels, where Charlotte had been until recently. Anne was worried, Emily was angry, and Charlotte was upset. Mr. Brontë sounded angry, too. They all seemed to think the letter was from a man, but Anne's idea that it was maybe from the man's wife had been met with even more horror. *What could be in that letter?* wondered Carly. In her experience letters were fun: You got them on your birthday and from your favorite cousin who lived in Virginia. They didn't make everyone in the house panic.

What was *wrong* with the Brontës, anyway? A little girl had died and they were all in a flutter over a *letter*? Carly started to feel angry. It was stupid. They should be worried about the Martins, not some people in Brussels. In Carly's opinion, this was no way to behave, no matter how good a language teacher Charlotte was.

Carly crashed her hands down on the piano keys. Charlotte was a grown-up. If she didn't want her dad to read her letter, then he shouldn't. Maybe she should go tell them so.

As Carly banged the lid of the piano closed, Anne appeared in the doorway.

"Ah, Caroline. There you are. Are you coming to lunch?"

She couldn't sweep down the stairs in righteous indignation if Anne was with her. Deflated, Carly followed her to the dining room. She could tell the Brontë sisters what she thought of their childish behavior over lunch.

But her plan was thwarted by the simple fact that no one was at lunch but herself and Anne.

"Where is everyone?" she asked.

"My sister Emily has gone for a walk on the moors. My father is taking lunch in his study. Charlotte is with him. And Branwell is resting upstairs with a headache," said Anne, not looking at Carly while she spoke.

"I'll bet he has a 'headache'," muttered Carly, thinking of the bottle Branwell had absconded with from the cupboard.

"What did you say?" asked Anne.

"I said, 'I hope Branwell is okay,'" said Carly untruthfully.

"I thought Charlotte had spoken to you about your shocking language?" said Anne with a pointed look. "And I'm sure Branwell will be fully recovered by tomorrow morning. He is of a delicate constitution, you know."

Carly had nothing to say to that: it seemed impolite to flatly contradict Anne. They ate in silence. Lunch was peas and thick slices of bread with cheese and leftover mutton. Carly watched Anne closely—she did not eat much, but pushed the food around on her plate.

"So," said Carly, trying to sound casual. "Who was the letter from?"

Anne froze, fork halfway to her mouth.

"That is none of your concern," she said.

Carly shrugged. "It certainly caused a fuss. I was just curious."

Anne set her fork down very precisely.

"You may go fetch your history book now," she said. "Sit in here to read it. Tabby is going to clean the school room this afternoon." Her tone was decidedly frosty.

But how am I supposed to learn anything without asking questions?

That afternoon, Carly tried to pay attention to the history book—she really did. But it was written in so old-fashioned a tone that it sucked all the life out of even the most exciting and interesting events. Carly had not thought it possible to make the Spanish Armada sound *boring*. She found herself staring at the fire more and more, and reading less and less.

Her initial annoyance at being left out of all the interesting events gave way to concern for Charlotte. Even if Charlotte hadn't been surprised by the death of Bridget Martin, she had still been saddened. What must it be like to live in a time when a child's death was an everyday occurrence?

Carly shivered and moved her chair closer to the fire. She didn't want to be stuck here, to have to worry about dying from things like typhoid or tuberculosis. Yes, she liked the clothes and the old-fashioned manners and the way everyone talked (even if she forgot and used modern slang). Yes, the moors were very beautiful—but they existed in the twenty-first century. Carly decided she would rather go visit them with her parents and brother and Francesca than live on them in 1846.

With a dramatic sigh, Carly started reading her history book again. She didn't want Charlotte to come in and find her daydreaming by the fire. Realizing she hadn't taken in any of what she'd already read that day, she turned to the beginning of the section with a groan.

Finally, Carly had to stand up and stretch her legs. It felt as though she'd been sitting for hours. Walking slowly around the table, she looked at the clock on the mantelpiece. Almost four o'clock! Time hadn't exactly flown, but it was late enough that Carly felt justified in closing her history text with a thump.

It's weird Charlotte never came to see what I was doing, Carly thought, still walking around the table. *I hope she's okay.* Carly paused and put her hand on the back of the chair that was Charlotte's. Her governess had been so upset earlier, and she hadn't checked on Carly in hours—neither had anyone else. Usually they would have been gathering for tea by now.

Carly poked her head out into the hallway. Nothing. She walked quietly over to the door of Mr. Brontë's study and leaned in close. No noise. She crept down the hall to the kitchen doorway and listened again. *Jackpot.* Emily was talking to Martha, the maid of all work who came in daily to help Tabby.

"She didn't eat any lunch, you say? Well, I'll help you prepare dinner and then go find her. She can't starve herself. Anne took Father a cup of tea, and the rest of us can hold out till dinner."

Carly went quickly upstairs and checked the room she and Charlotte shared. No one. She poked her head into the schoolroom, not really expecting to see Charlotte in there, but wanting to be thorough. She gave the closed door of Mr. Brontë and Branwell's room a wide berth.

I bet she's in the garden, thought Carly. *That's where I'd go if I wanted to be alone.* Without waiting to put on a coat or shawl, Carly slipped out of the house.

When she found Charlotte, she wished she hadn't.

Coming around a bend in the path, Carly almost tripped over Charlotte, who sat on the ground, crumpled forward with her arms and head leaning against a stone bench beside the path. Her skirt pooled around her. Charlotte was crying bitterly—not ladylike sniffles or restrained weeping, but wracking, ugly sobs that shook her whole body.

Carly tried to back up around the corner without being noticed, but Charlotte looked up at the sound of her footsteps. When she saw Charlotte's blotched face, Carly couldn't stop herself from saying, "Oh, my gosh, are you okay?"

"What do you think?" retorted Charlotte, almost incomprehensibly. "What do you think?" she said again, sounding angrier.

"Umm . . . No?" guessed Carly, still edging backwards.

Charlotte struggled to her feet and took Carly's arm.

"Of course I'm not all right, you . . . you . . ." she shook Carly, then continued. "Everywhere I go I am reminded of him. Everywhere!" She broke off in a sob.

"Isn't he married? To someone else?" asked Carly, guessing the truth from what she'd heard on the stairs.

Charlotte slapped Carly full across the face and then fell onto the bench, still crying. Carly stumbled backwards, a hand to her stinging cheek, shocked to her core. No one had ever hit her before. How could Charlotte, of all people, do this to her? Hot tears welled up in her eyes.

Blindly, she ran back into the house. She wanted to hide in her room. But her room was also Charlotte's. What if Charlotte came in and yelled at her or slapped her again? But there was nowhere else where she could count on even a little privacy.

Carly kept climbing the stairs, trying very hard not to cry. Her cheek hurt so much she worried she was getting a black eye. There wasn't even any ice to put on it. *Stupid Victorian Era, with your stupid lack of refrigeration*, she thought. She wanted to be home. She wanted to leave this place and this time. Adventures weren't supposed to be like this. What was *wrong* with this family?

Whatever it was, Carly couldn't fix it. Unable to hold back the tears any longer, she cradled her cheek in her hand and cried as she climbed the stairs.

She was so upset she didn't hear the door to Branwell's room open. When his hand reached out and grabbed her arm at the exact point where Charlotte had held it, Carly was so scared she almost fell backwards down the stairs. But Branwell's grip was too tight.

"Having fun?" he asked, his eyes fever-bright.

"No!" sobbed Carly, crying harder. "No, I want to go home!"

"You think you're so clever, coming here to spy on me. But I know what you're doing. You can't fool me! You'll never fool me, never!" Branwell shouted.

"What are you talking about? I'm not spying on you!" Carly shouted back, shocked into speech. She wasn't sure Branwell could even hear her or knew who she was. That mad gleam from the other night was back in his eyes.

"Let go of me!" she cried, trying to free her arm.

"Branwell!" shouted Emily, appearing at the foot of the stairs. "Branwell, stop!"

Anne, with Mr. Brontë next to her, emerged from the study and followed Emily upstairs. Emily put a soothing hand on Branwell's arm, which held Carly so tightly.

"Let her go, Branwell. It's Caroline, Charlotte's pupil."

Anne ran ahead of her father up the stairs and stood behind Carly.

"Yes, Branwell. I'll take her away if you just let her go," she said.

Branwell hesitated. Carly tried to choke back her tears for fear of setting him off again.

"Come, Branwell, let me help you to bed. You are not well," said Emily in commanding tones. Branwell released Carly, and it was only as Anne was leading her towards her own room that Carly saw Mr. Brontë was brandishing a revolver.

"He has a gun! Why does he have a gun?"

"Never mind. It will all be well soon. Come this way," said Anne, hurrying her into her room.

As Anne shut the door, Carly heard Emily snap, "Oh, put that away, Father; you'll only shoot the wrong person."

Weak from fright, Carly let Anne help undress her and tuck her into bed.

"I'll bring you tea and bread and jam soon," said Anne. "Rest until I return."

"Don't let them come in here, please. Please don't," said Carly, no longer trying to hold back sobs.

Anne looked at the red mark on Carly's face. "Did Branwell hit you?" she asked.

"No," said Carly. "Charlotte did. Why would she do that to me? I want my mom. I want to go home!" Tears again overwhelmed her. Carly had thought that Charlotte liked her, that she was on her side. Carly wasn't sure what hurt more, her cheek or her feelings. After the way Charlotte had encouraged her at her lessons and trusted her enough to talk about how difficult things were with Branwell, how could she lose it like that? Carly burrowed further under the covers, trying to make herself as small as possible.

"There, there," said Anne. "She and Branwell are not themselves today. You will be safe tucked up here in bed. Try to rest."

Carly buried her face in her pillow and cried harder. It was all too much—the ghostly girl, Charlotte's anger, Branwell's unpredictable behavior . . . and Anne was acting like it was okay for your governess to hit you. Carly felt horribly alone. How could Anne—gentle, kind Anne—excuse Charlotte and Branwell's behavior as if they were just acting grumpy? Carly wanted to be home where people didn't hit you for no reason or yell at you for asking questions or wave guns around. 1846 was the *worst*.

After a final pat to her shoulder, Anne went out, closing the door behind her.

CHAPTER SEVEN

Carly slept fitfully through the late afternoon and night. Each time she awoke, still frightened, she was alone—Charlotte did not sleep in their room that night. Each time Carly dropped back to sleep, she had confused and ominous dreams. First one and then another of the Brontës chased her around the graveyard, shouting that Carly had not learned her lesson and was good for nothing so they might as well get rid of her. Each wanted to do this differently: Mr. Brontë brandished his pistol; Branwell kept holding up the bottle of laudanum and urging her to drink poison; Emily insisted that freezing to death lost on the moors was the romantic way to go; Charlotte tried to squash Carly like a bug with her French grammar; every so often, Anne would pop up from behind a tombstone and sigh, "Life would be *so* much easier if you would just *go*."

Finally, Carly could take no more. She got up, wrapped herself in a warm shawl, and sat looking out her window at the dim dawn. Slowly, the view extended as the light brightened. At first the earth was all black shapes and stars still shone in the sky. Then more of the sky was grey, and Carly could see the shapes of trees and hedges—still black but now distinct—emerging against the patchwork of fields that lay against the moors.

Still she sat by the window and watched. Not for anything in particular, but because she missed home and her family—and because she was frightened of what the next day would bring. Branwell was obviously unwell, but the fact that Charlotte, who always seemed so in control, could be driven to hysterics scared Carly. Her cheek hurt where Charlotte had slapped her, and her arm was tender where Branwell had gripped it. What was wrong with these Brontës? Or maybe everyone in 1846 thought it was A-okay to slap children?

Carly was dreading facing Charlotte again. What would she say if Charlotte apologized? Was she ready to forgive her? What if Charlotte didn't apologize? Should Carly tell her how wrong she thought it was to hit people, especially kids?

Most of all, though, Carly wanted to avoid Branwell—she got a trickle of dread down her spine remembering his wild words of the day before.

She leaned her head on the windowpane and wondered for the hundredth time why she was here. Had the old man at the bookshop *known* what would happen? If so, he might have given her some warning, Carly thought indignantly. And if he hadn't sent her, then how in heaven's name had she ended up here? Carly had read plenty of books in front of a fire and never been transported anywhere.

Carly sighed. Would anyone, even Francesca, believe her when she got home? *If* she got home, since she was no closer than before to figuring out how to get there . . .

Wait!

The armchair by the fire! She hadn't tried it before because she hadn't been ready for her adventure to end, but *now*? Now she'd be happy to get home. She stood and clutched her shawl more closely about her shoulders. She'd try it immediately.

There was just enough light to see her way dimly across the room. Softly, Carly opened the door, stole down the stairs, and slipped into Mr. Brontë's study. There was no fire in the grate, but Carly hoped it wouldn't matter. After her restless night she was tired enough to fall asleep without the warmth and light of flames.

Carly practically hopped into the chair in which she'd awoken a few days before and laid her head down. It popped back up. This was so exciting, to be about to be magically transported home! Carly squirmed around to get more comfortable. She closed her eyes—and heard a slight noise! She was home!

Nope, she was in Mr. Brontë's study. Carly closed her eyes again. This time, she said to herself, *I won't open them until I can tell something has happened.* She kept her eyes closed for what seemed like ages. She peeked quickly with one eye, her eyelid barely cracked open. No change.

Carly let out a big sigh. What could be taking so long? Maybe she needed to ask to go home. She squeezed her eyes tight shut.

"Please, I'd like to go home now."

Carly waited. She opened her eyes and looked around. The cold fireplace of Mr. Brontë's study looked back at her. This time when Carly closed her eyes, it was because hot tears were pricking at them and she didn't want to cry. She sat very still and tried not to mind that she remained at Haworth. To think of all those times she'd fallen asleep in front of fires or walked into large cupboards or wardrobes, only to be disappointed not to enter a magical kingdom! She'd never been trying to get *out* of an adventure before.

"*Why?*" she whispered.

"Trapped," rasped a voice in her ear. "You're all trapped."

Carly sat bolt upright. Next to her, barely visible against the dawn light, was the girl from the night before. Carly gave a gasp of fright. The girl raised her skeleton-like hand and pointed at Carly.

"There is no hope if you do not free them," she whispered. Chills chased up and down Carly's spine. The raspy whisper of the ghost's voice gave Carly exactly the same feeling she had when a giant brown bear appeared out of the forest: a burst of adrenaline combined with a paralyzing, primal fear. The ghost made Carly's heart race and her whole body tense, ready for fight or flight. At home Carly loved to read books with ghosts in them and never found them very scary. But until now she had never met one. It turned out the books had left her woefully unprepared.

"Who—What—" stammered out Carly.

Without a sound, the ghost faded away into the dim morning light, leaving Carly trembling from the adrenaline.

The study door opened and Tabby entered.

"Land's sakes, Miss Caroline, you gave me a fright! What are you doing up so early? I just got here myself to light the fires and put a kettle on."

Carly couldn't reply; she was still too alarmed to speak. Tabby didn't wait long before she continued, "You'll catch your death of cold in this drafty house in naught but your night-gown and a shawl. If you can't sleep, which is no wonder for those not bred up on the moor, then you'd better come into the kitchen and sit by the stove to keep warm. I'll let you have a slice of bread and butter as soon as the bread's out of the oven."

Tabby's soothing prattle allowed Carly to find her voice again. "Sometimes I can't sleep. I just need to think about things."

"Eh, you'd think you were another Brontë with your ways—always wanting bread and apples in a handkerchief so's they can walk for hours on the moors. Miss Emily is the worst."

Relieved to be around someone who was neither a ghost nor inclined to hit her, Carly followed Tabby to the kitchen. After watching her put the bread in to bake (how did she know how hot the oven was with no dial to set it, or thermometer?), and getting a hot slice with plenty of butter half an hour later, Carly went back upstairs to dress. What did the ghost mean when she said that Carly was trapped?

She opened the door of her room and saw a teary-eyed Charlotte hastily shove something in the top drawer of the bureau. Carly pretended not to notice, walked stiffly over, and sat on the edge of the bed. *She* wasn't going to be the first to speak.

Charlotte turned an apparently calm face to Carly.

"Caroline, you are up early. I ought not to have struck you while I was so upset yesterday. I was . . . not myself. I make it a rule only to strike my pupils when they display a shocking want of discipline."

Carly felt a flare of anger at Charlotte and touched her cheek lightly.

"I am sorry if it still pains you," said Charlotte, noticing the gesture.

Unwilling to voice her anger and hurt for fear of provoking another fight, and intimidated by the memory of Charlotte's hysteria the day before, Carly nodded tentatively.

"Now," said Charlotte, briskly. "Get dressed for the day before you catch your death of cold."

Understanding that Charlotte would not talk any more about the day before, Carly lay out her clothing for the day while taking some deep, calming breaths: drawers, stockings, petticoats, dress, pinafore, hair ribbon, shoes. She had a pretty good guess what Charlotte had hidden in the bureau drawer, and she wanted to get a look at it.

Carly spent breakfast puzzling out the best time to sneak upstairs to look for the letter. She didn't want Charlotte to have time to move it to a better hiding spot. Just before lunch, she decided.

Like the last time he'd been so creepy, Branwell wasn't at breakfast. Carly was happy about that. She didn't think Charlotte was likely to hit her again any time soon, but she placed no such reliance on Branwell. Why his sisters seemed to dote on him, she could not understand. He was selfish and unhelpful around the house—not to mention mean and paranoid when he was having one of his episodes. How disappointing after her original excitement at the idea of an older brother. It made Carly thankful for James, even if he could be super annoying sometimes.

Carly tried hard to pay attention to her geography lesson—but she kept sneaking looks at the clock until it was time for lunch. When the hands reached half-past eleven o'clock, Carly took out her handkerchief and blew her nose, twice. Feigning surprise, she said, "Gross! I'd better go get a new handkerchief," and hopped out of her chair.

Charlotte, who had stood to take Carly down to lunch, started to say something, but Carly held the hankie between two fingers and waved it at her.

"I'll meet you in the dining room as soon as I get a clean handkerchief. This one is disgusting."

Before Charlotte could object, Carly ran out of the room and across the hall. She paused and listened. Good, Charlotte was going downstairs. Quickly, Carly tiptoed to the bureau. Charlotte had been messing with the top drawer, so Carly pulled it open and started digging through the contents, trying not to disturb things too much.

A-ha! Her fingers touched paper and she carefully drew out the letter. It wasn't very thick, thought Carly, unfolding it gingerly, like it might bite. Immediately she saw that it was only one piece of paper—the letter writer had written down the page, the way anyone would, and then had apparently turned the piece of paper sideways and written the rest of his letter the other way. The closely crossed lines looked like someone's doodles; Carly squinted, trying to make her eyes read one set of lines and ignore the others for now.

Worse and worse! The letter was in French! Carly was so disappointed that she groaned aloud. Without any real hope of success, she turned the letter ninety degrees and tried to scan the written lines of the second part. A word jumped out at her: *English.* She slowed down and looked more closely. Here is what she read:

"I repeat this in your native English so there can be no possibility of misunderstanding: I cannot return your regard, so tenderly given. You must think of me no more. Everything forbids it—prudence, the duty owed my wife, your future duty to the man so fortunate as to win your hand, and even the talents that make you such an able practitioner of the literary arts. Think of me no more—put from yourself reflections which can increase neither your happiness nor your respectability."

No wonder Charlotte was so upset! Carly shook her head as she slipped the letter back into the drawer. Guiltily, she realized that she had invaded Charlotte's privacy terribly. *Well, she shouldn't have hit me*, thought Carly, uncomfortably aware that two wrongs did not make a right.

Trying to look innocent, Carly ran down the stairs to the dining room. To take her mind off her guilty conscience, she watched Mr. Brontë fish gently about his plate for bites of lunch. Carly wondered what she'd do if her dad was as autocratic as Mr. Brontë. She couldn't imagine he'd make her read a private letter out loud, especially if she was as old as Charlotte. Carly turned her attention to the rest of the table.

Anne and Emily were arguing about the best words to capture the color of the moors at twilight. Charlotte listened with half an ear, but did not speak. Beside his sisters, Branwell looked pale and haggard, and he had dark circles under his eyes. Carly remembered the feel of his hand gripping her arm too well to feel any pity. *Serves him right for being so mean*, she thought. *I hope he has one heck of a headache.*

Branwell, as if sensing her hostile scrutiny, looked up from his plate and stared at Carly with as much dislike in his gaze as Carly had in hers. *He looks haunted!* Carly thought. She stifled a bitter giggle as she speared some beans with her fork. *But really, I'm the one who should look haunted!*

With that, her mind turned from Branwell back to the mystery of the ghost and the spirit's inscrutable words. Who needed saving? What would happen to her if she didn't do what the ghost commanded? Carly shivered, remembering the skeletal hand raised accusingly at her.

When they had finished lunch, Charlotte and Carly went back upstairs to the study, where Charlotte arranged several books on the table.

"Today we will turn from the modern languages to literature. Every young lady ought to be well read, so to begin you will read aloud from *The Pilgrim's Progress*."

Carly attempted to hide her dismay. She had tried to read *The Pilgrim's Progress* after reading *Little Women* because the March sisters all seemed to like it so much, but she had found the seventeenth-century allegory unbelievably dull and abandoned it after only a few pages.

Rather than starting to read right away, she looked over at Charlotte and said, "Why don't you and your sisters have the school I've heard you talk about? You know so much, all of you! I don't see why parents wouldn't be happy to send their children to you. Why did your other school fail?"

Charlotte looked down at the table and gave a melancholy sigh.

"Well, it didn't fail precisely. We never opened it," she said.

"Why not?" asked Carly.

Through the open door, they saw Branwell come up the stairs and go into his room. Charlotte sighed again.

"Oh," said Carly. "Well, I don't see why having a badly-behaved brother should have anything to do with whether you and Miss Anne and Miss Emily are good teachers."

"It is not so simple as that," said Charlotte. "You are too young, perhaps, to understand the very great influence one's family can have on one's reputation, particularly a woman's reputation."

"That's stupid. It's not like Branwell was going to be teaching there, was he?"

"No, it was to be the three of us sisters," said Charlotte.

"So was the whole problem that people didn't like Branwell?"

"I realize that Branwell's behavior towards you has not been what it ought . . ."

Carly snorted under her breath. Charlotte continued as if she hadn't heard.

"But that does not mean you should speak so rudely of someone both older than you and not of your family."

"You're right: His behavior has been horrible," said Carly, unwilling to let the subject go. "But that doesn't mean I think you're a worse teacher! It doesn't make sense to punish the three of you for his mistakes."

"It is the way of the world," said Charlotte. "While that ought not to affect us, I am afraid our courage was not equal to risking society's scorn for disappointed hopes. Nothing is gained by dwelling on the past, however. I assure you that my sisters and I are quite reconciled to the loss of our school."

Carly raised her eyebrows skeptically. "Yes, Miss Emily always sounds really *reconciled* when she talks about it."

Even Charlotte, in her melancholy state, was obliged to smile at that.

"Emily has never been the most . . . forgiving member of the family. But she loves Branwell for all that."

"I still think people shouldn't refuse to send their kids to you just because your brother's a . . ."

Charlotte interrupted her hastily: "I believe you were going to begin reading *The Pilgrim's Progress* aloud, Caroline. Please try to speak clearly and place the proper emphasis on the words."

Carly was about to protest that Charlotte shouldn't care what other people said, but remembered her own insistence to Francesca that French Camp was too scary to even apply. There would be time to ponder Charlotte's words and to worry about the ghost after lessons, but she didn't think Charlotte would brook any more delays. Deciding to let it be for the moment, Carly opened the book to the first chapter.

"As I walked through the wilderness of this world, I lighted in a certain place where was a den, and laid me down in that place to sleep . . ."

CHAPTER EIGHT

Carly waited nervously for the ghost to reappear. She waited through the first several chapters of *The Pilgrim's Progress*. She waited through piano practice and dinner. She waited while Emily played piano for her, Charlotte, and Anne after dinner, and Mr. Brontë and Branwell retired to Mr. Brontë's study.

Emily was very good, Carly had to admit—when she stopped looking over her shoulder long enough to listen.

Much to her relief, there had been no sign of the ghost by the time she went up to bed to read. Eventually the candle guttered in its holder and Carly couldn't keep her eyes open another minute. The room was cold but there was a hot brick under the covers. As long as she was snuggled under the blankets, Carly was warm enough. She drifted off to sleep, listening to the sound of Charlotte, Emily, and Anne walking around and around the table in the dining room. Her last thought was: maybe it's someone else's turn to be haunted.

In the morning, it was a pleasant surprise to realize that it was Saturday and there would only be a drawing lesson along with some botany out in the garden. The weather was mild. While Charlotte could not be called cheerful, she was at least not so melancholy as Carly had seen her for the past two days. Some of her usual equanimity had returned; maybe she'd gotten over the shock and realized Monsieur Heger wasn't worth pining over. *Or at least I hope so,* thought Carly.

After spending the morning with Charlotte—punctuated by visits from Anne (to gather herbs from the kitchen garden) and Emily (as she returned from a walk)—Carly realized that she spent so little time alone that it would be difficult for the ghost to haunt her even if it wished to do so. So far, it had shown no inclination to show itself to the other people in the house. In the absence of the ghost, Carly's courage was rising and she almost wished it would appear just so she could give it a piece of her mind about scaring innocent people for no good reason.

Over a lunch of trout one of Mr. Brontë's parishioners had brought, Emily complained of having forgotten to pick some heather to put in the linen closet during her morning walk on the moors.

"It is so vexing, because I shan't have time to do it this afternoon, what with the household accounts," said Emily in a discontented tone.

"I'd be happy to go and get some heather," volunteered Carly, willing to risk the ghost if it meant some time alone outside. She saw the look Emily gave Charlotte and hastily added: "My parents never objected to my walking at home."

"It is very mild today," said Anne.

"I promise to stay on the path and not wander, so you don't need to worry I'll get lost," said Carly, trying to anticipate any objections Charlotte might have.

"Very well, then. And . . . thank you for saying you will do it. It would have been inconvenient for any of us this afternoon," said Charlotte, bestowing a smile of approval on Carly.

"If you give me a moment after we finish, I will fetch you a knife so you can cut the stems—they are quite tough," said Anne.

"Two or three bunches ought to be enough," Emily added.

Carly quickly finished lunch and went to get her bonnet—funny how after only five days with the Brontës she was already used to remembering things like that. Anne brought her a small knife and a flat wicker basket in which to put the heather.

Charlotte insisted she take a snack of bread and cheese and an apple, in case she felt hungry. More cheerful than she'd felt in days, Carly set off through the garden and out the back gate onto the moor. Eagerly she broke out of the trees, swinging her basket as she walked. Carly decided not to pick the first heather she came across, but to get a good walk in while she had the chance.

"The only thing waiting for me back at the house is more piano practice. Ugh, I've never had to practice so much in my life! Girls had a pretty dull time of it in 1846, although the botany's interesting. Mom will be impressed that I know the names of so many plants now!" said Carly aloud to herself.

CARLY KEENE: LITERARY DETECTIVE

The thought of her mother temporarily quelled Carly's high spirits, and she walked on in a more introspective mood. What was her family doing right now? she wondered. Were they frozen in time, still cutting up James' cohos?

As she rambled, Carly made sure to stay on the path, which wasn't much more than a sheep track. She didn't pay close attention to the direction in which it meandered, but Carly wasn't scared of getting lost. The moors were open, and even if one hollow hid the horizon from view, the path soon climbed upwards again.

It was not so late in the season that fall had a tight hold— the heather still waved happily; some even had purple blooms. Emily had told Carly that the moor plant started blooming in late summer. Carly saw a few larks darting around the sky, and bees closer by in the heather. She made plenty of noise with her feet in case adders were lurking on the path—a useful tip she'd learned from her favorite book, *Swallows and Amazons.* Along the horizon, the sky was hazy, but up high it was blue, blue, blue, just like in *The Secret Garden.* Carly wished that there were a Dickon around to make friends with—it would be so nice to have someone her own age!—then turned again to business.

"I must go about this logically," she said aloud. "First, the problems: one, I don't know how to get home; two, I'm being haunted by a ghost, but the ghost hasn't told me why; three, Charlotte has a terrible brother and she's in love with a married man in Brussels. Which is kind of shocking," she finished, raising her eyebrows to herself.

"I can't do anything about the fact that he's married . . . but maybe there's someone else." Even though she was still angry at Charlotte for hitting her, Carly's mind filled with visions of matchmaking. She would find a suitable gentleman and introduce him to Charlotte! He would appreciate her wit and writing ability and be instantly smitten. Sure, Charlotte thought she could never love again, but slowly, after some subtle mentions from Carly about the man's suitability as a husband, her wounded heart would be healed.

Carly sighed happily at the thought of bringing about such a romantic resolution to Charlotte's heartache, like Ron did with Harry and Ginny. Only *she* would do more than give Charlotte a book on failsafe ways to charm witches. She just needed to find the right gentleman.

Maybe that tall one—Mr. Nicholls—whom she and Charlotte had seen yesterday at the Martins'? Carly thought his side-whiskers silly, but Mr. Brontë and Branwell also had them, so Charlotte probably wouldn't mind. And he'd been very kind about walking them home.

Satisfied that she had come up with a good plan to heal Charlotte's broken heart, Carly decided she couldn't be expected to do anything about Branwell. Plus, she found him too scary to want to try. Thinking over her other problems, Carly could see nothing she could do about either until she had more information or a chance to actually talk to the ghost instead of being threatened in vague terms.

Scuffing her shoes idly along, Carly gave a shiver. The day had been mild with no breeze, but Carly realized she was cold; the damp chilliness reminded her of fall in Juneau. She looked around and was startled to see that the broad views were gone. She could see no further than the nearest hill. As she watched, fog covered that too. Within thirty seconds, Carly could see nothing that wasn't a couple feet ahead.

Should she try finding her way back along the path? Carly thought nervously. No; she had noticed several smaller sheep tracks branching off as she walked, and if she took one by mistake, she would be in real trouble. For now, the best thing would be to stay where she was—it wouldn't be dark for hours yet, and the fog couldn't last forever. Getting back would be much easier if she could see where she was going.

Resigned to a period of inactivity, Carly walked a few feet back to a rock sticking out of a clump of heather next to the trail. Taking out the knife, she cut some of the heather for her basket. How much was a few bunches, she wondered? She cut more. Better to have too much than not enough.

Her task finished, Carly sat down on the rock to wait. For something to do, she ate her apple, taking very small bites to see if she could make it last longer than the fog.

When nothing but a bit of core was left, the fog was as heavy as ever. Carly threw the core as hard as she could into the mist. Throwing apple cores probably wasn't one of the accomplishments Charlotte would call indispensable for a young lady, but Carly didn't care. It was more fun than most of the other things she got to do at the parsonage.

Sitting around like this was boring. Carly sighed, loudly and tried some owl sounds, "hoo-hoo"-ing into the fog. As she was drawing in another breath, the hair on the back of her neck stood up, and Carly heard a sigh in the fog-muffled air. But instead of the fear that had gripped her on previous occasions, Carly felt anger burning the fear right out.

"No!" she shouted, jumping to her feet. "Stop it! Stop it right now! Show yourself and just . . . cut it out!"

To her astonishment, the ghostly girl appeared beside her, looking almost pleased.

"You must save them," she said.

"Shut up!" Carly was on a roll. "Stop saying that until you tell me who you are and what you want. I can't save anyone, including myself, if you don't tell me what's going on!"

"You are trapped here until you help my sisters," said the ghost.

"Are you threatening me?"

"No!" exclaimed the girl, her sunken eyes widening in shock at the idea. "No one else will listen to me or even acknowledge I'm here, but you, you can help me."

Carly took a minute to look the girl over. Now that she had appeared in the daylight, Carly could see that she was about the same age as Carly herself, but the ghost was very thin and sickly. Her long, light brown hair hung limply around her gaunt face; hollow eyes with heavy shadows under them stared at Carly with painful intensity.

"You want me to help you?" asked Carly, responding to the intensity of the girl's gaze.

"Yes."

"Then why didn't you *say* that instead of scaring me half to death?" Carly narrowed her eyes in exasperation. "I thought you wanted to kill me!"

"Kill you?" said the ghost, looking startled.

"If ghosts are part of the adventure, fine," said Carly. She shook her finger sternly at the specter. "But no more scaring me half to death. Tell me what you need."

"Then listen well; I do not have much time. You *must* save my sisters. They do not have much time, either."

"Are they ghosts too?" asked Carly sympathetically. "What's your name?"

"They are not ghosts—they are alive and need your help. My name is Maria . . ." The girl hesitated for a moment. "Maria Brontë."

Carly gasped. "I didn't know Charlotte had another sister!"

"There isn't time to tell you the whole sad tale," said Maria. "What matters is that you help them. Only then will you be free to return home."

"Okay, so tell me what to do. How do I free your sisters?"

Maria looked searchingly at Carly. "You should know it will not be easy."

Carly almost scoffed. "Of course not. That's the whole point of an adventure."

"It is simple, but not easy," repeated Maria.

"So tell me," said Carly, starting to get impatient with the girl's vague pronouncements.

"You must make sure *they* tell their stories—and then *you* must read *Jane Eyre*," said the ghost. "The only way to return is the way you arrived, but it will only work if my sisters experience the catharsis of writing *Wuthering Heights*, *Agnes Grey*, and . . ."

Carly interrupted her.

"That's right! I'd just started reading *Jane Eyre* by the fire when I woke up here! Of course I have to read it to go back. Great! No problem!"

In her excitement, Carly leapt to her feet and danced around, flinging her arms out into the fog. Maria regarded her with some consternation.

"I don't think you understand," she started—but then the loud sound of hooves on the turf thundered out of the fog.

Maria and Carly whirled to see where the noise was coming from. A huge horse loomed out of the mists along the path. Maria gave a gasp and disappeared. Carly gave a scream, and the horse reared. Its rider was thrown and landed with a curse on the ground. Fortunately, his horse decided not to bolt, but instead lowered its head and snuffled, first at its master and then at Carly.

Carly, her heart racing from fright, walked closer. Despite her long-held view that horses were twitchy and not to be trusted, she took hold of the reins. She and the horse looked down at the man who was struggling to get his wind back: Mr. Nicholls.

"Are you all right?" asked Carly.

"What the dev—blazes do you think? What a stupid thing to do, leaping out at us like that! I might have broken my leg, or worse, my horse might have," said the curate, getting gingerly to his feet.

"I didn't leap out at you! I've been sitting here for hours," said Carly, somewhat inaccurately. "And it's a pretty stupid thing to be riding so fast in the fog, I think!"

Mr. Nicholls gave a short bark of laughter as he brushed himself off.

"Impertinent, aren't you? Here, give me those," he said, taking the reins. "To where do you belong?" he asked.

Carly felt like saying "Alaska" just to startle him, but decided it wasn't worth the questions.

"I need to get back to Haworth, but I didn't want to lose my way, so I'm waiting here until the fog lifts."

"Ah, yes, you're Miss Brontë's new charge," he said. Carly thought this too obvious to need any reply, considering that she'd seen him at the Martins' so recently.

"I'd best take you back on my horse so you don't break some other rider's neck. And I can tell Miss Brontë what an impudent pupil she has."

Carly didn't take his threat very seriously as it was said without the least heat. *Excellent*, she thought, *he has a sense of humor—indispensable in a husband according to all my favorite books.* "Are you sure you know the way?" she asked.

"Of course. Are you this rude to all your elders?" Mr. Nicholls said.

"I don't think so," said Carly, not completely sure what he meant.

"Besides, the fog is lifting," he continued. "Come over to this rock. I'll mount, and then you can stand on the stone and I'll pull you up behind me."

"I have a basket of heather," Carly said, hoping she wouldn't have to try to ride the tall horse.

"Of course you do," said Mr. Nicholls with a sigh, raising his eyebrows.

"I should probably walk," said Carly, edging away. "I don't mind."

"Stop dilly-dallying and hand me the basket."

Understanding from his stern tone that there was no help for it, Carly managed to climb up behind him (the horse looked askance at the proceedings but offered no objection beyond a few sidling steps). Proceeding at a decorous walk, they rode back to the parsonage.

For the first few minutes, Carly was too busy trying to stay on a horse in a dress to have any spare attention for talking. But the horse was very calm and Carly realized that riding wasn't as scary as she'd thought it would be—as long as they didn't go too fast.

"I'm sorry I startled your horse. I was . . . distracted by something and didn't think," said Carly to Mr. Nicholls' back.

"It might have been much worse, so no harm done," said Mr. Nicholls over his shoulder. "What is your name?"

"Carl—Caroline. Caroline Keene."

"Miss Keene. Good. I like to know the names of people I almost ride down in fogs."

Carly began to quite like Mr. Nicholls, despite his side-whiskers. Her earlier impulse was right, she thought: He would definitely be a good husband for Charlotte. She decided to test the waters.

"How well do you know Miss Brontë?"

"She and I see quite a lot of each other due to her father's eye troubles. I imagine she is an admirable governess."

"Oh, yes," said Carly, wondering whether men often wanted to marry women who made "admirable governesses."

Before she knew it, they were at the parsonage. Mr. Nicholls held her basket while she slipped down from the horse, and then handed it back to her.

"I was already here this morning, so I shan't come in. Please give my greetings to the family," he said with a smile.

"I will. Sorry again for making you fall off your horse," said Carly, feeling bold enough to put out a hand for the horse to snuffle at.

"Serves me right for hurrying in a fog," said Mr. Nicholls, tipping his hat to Carly. "Goodbye."

"Goodbye," said Carly.

As soon as she opened the door, Charlotte accosted her. Carly related how careful she had been to stay on the path so she wouldn't get lost, and then told of her adventure with Mr. Nicholls. Emily came out of the kitchen and listened to the tale.

"You're lucky he didn't break his leg or his neck," she said.

"I know," said Carly. "But he shouldn't have been riding that fast in such a fog."

Emily shrugged her shoulders, but Charlotte agreed.

"Yes, it would be all too easy to break a bone if you were thrown unexpectedly. I am glad neither you nor Mr. Nicholls were injured and that you are not lost on the moor!"

Carly smiled briefly at this, but wanted to be done with the subject so she could ponder what Maria had told her. Should she mention Maria to Charlotte and Emily? No, they already thought she was kind of crazy. Better to puzzle it out alone for now and then carry out the rescue as Maria intended. Carly smiled again, this time with the benevolence of someone who plans to heroically rescue the people at whom they are smiling. Emily and Charlotte looked in no way reassured.

"I think you had better lie down until dinner, Caroline," said Charlotte. "You look a trifle tired."

Carly was not tired, but she did have a lot to think about, so she made no demur about being sent to her room. She wanted to help the Brontë sisters because she liked them (despite their views on corporal punishment), and because she didn't like their sadness. But even more than that, she wanted desperately to get home so she could play What Would Hermione Do? with Francesca, finally drink some hot cocoa—and even give James a hug. If helping free the Brontës from their tortured past was how she could do it, then she would free them whether they wanted to be freed or not.

⇜ CHAPTER NINE ⇝

Carly sat with her back against the headboard, her knees drawn up to her chest. So. She could only get home the way she'd come, could she? Well, she'd already tried sitting in the armchair in which she'd awoken, with no results. Based on what Maria had said, that meant it had to be the book.

Jane Eyre. Carly scratched her ear absently. Charlotte had written it, so they had to have a copy somewhere. Carly couldn't see how reading *Jane Eyre* and telling the sisters to share their private stories would free them—*other than from me*, she thought, *which should suit Emily, at least.*

But Maria had been very clear: "You must make sure they tell their stories—and then you must read *Jane Eyre*." Carly knew from all the fairy tales she'd read that only bad things happened when you ignored the instructions of the old crone, the ghost, the wizard, the prophet, or the fairy godmother.

Carly had always been sure that if she were given a quest to complete, *she* would never do something so silly as ignore the directions of a magical helper. Well, here was her chance to show those nitwits from the fairy stories how adventures *ought* to be done. She'd probably be home by tomorrow morning.

The most efficient thing to do would be to find a copy of *Jane Eyre* before dinner, ask Charlotte, Emily, and Anne to tell her their tales over the meal, and then read *Jane Eyre* before she went to sleep. Nodding firmly, Carly climbed down from the bed and ran over to the bookshelf. It was not large, and part of each shelf held china figurines, so it didn't take long to determine that there was no copy of *Jane Eyre*. She tried to remember the first edition the old bookseller had given her. It was a red book, she thought, but the old man had said it ought to be blue. She'd look for both.

Rising, Carly went to the schoolroom. The only books there were tattered old things for lessons: grammars, foreign language dictionaries, a book on etiquette for young ladies (which Carly thought ought to be a book on etiquette for young gentlemen so Branwell could have profited from it), and a copy of that awful *Pilgrim's Progress*. She rustled through the cabinet where Branwell had hidden his bottle and looked behind the piano, but found nothing of interest.

Standing on the upper landing, she hesitated. Did she dare look through Anne and Emily's room—or Mr. Brontë and Branwell's? No, Carly decided; not yet. Instead, she'd have a quick look through Mr. Brontë's study.

Carly started down the stairs, but before she was halfway, Charlotte came to call her to dinner.

"Ah, Caroline, what exemplary punctuality!"

"I was just going to . . ." Carly trailed off. Well, she could wait to get a copy of *Jane Eyre* until after dinner. It didn't really matter in what order she accomplished Maria's tasks. She took her customary place at the dining table and sat, fidgeting her fingers. She could not immediately break into the conversation because Branwell and Mr. Brontë were discussing the sermon Mr. Brontë would deliver on Sunday. Branwell thought that his father was incorrectly interpreting a verse from the Gospel of John, but Charlotte and Anne sided with Mr. Brontë. Emily did not appear interested at all, so concentrated was she on her dinner. Carly didn't think turnips deserved such attention, although the chicken was nice.

She knew side conversations during meals were not encouraged, so she resisted the urge to talk across the table to Emily. Finally Branwell conceded defeat, and the talk grew more general. Seeing her moment, Carly used a lull in the conversation to say,

"So, now that I've been here a bit, why don't you tell me more about yourselves? I'd love to hear all about you."

The whole table froze. Five pairs of eyes turned on her. And not in an admiring way.

"What?" said Emily, a forkful of turnips frozen in mid-air.

"You know, how you're doing. Your hopes and dreams, that sort of thing," said Carly, feeling acutely uncomfortable but not willing to back down.

"Was she raised in a barn, do you think?" Emily asked Charlotte, turning to look at her sister.

"You certainly have your work cut out for you!" added Branwell, also looking accusingly at Charlotte. Anne said nothing, but stared fixedly at her plate. Mr. Brontë seemed too amazed to do more than stare.

Charlotte's lips thinned.

"Caroline, that is an entirely inappropriate question. I am shocked."

"Why?" asked Carly. "What's wrong with wanting to get to know you better? My grandmother says it's always important to enquire about your hosts. It makes you a better houseguest."

"While there is nothing amiss in your grandmother's sentiment, your overly bold way of speaking without invitation to do so deserves censure."

"So you don't care if I want to know you better, but you do care if I say so?" Carly wished again that people here would say what they meant instead of things like "deserves censure." She didn't even know that word!

Anne said in a gentle tone, "Such a way of putting your questions must seem like you wish to force the confidence of those you desire to know."

"It is also an entirely unsuitable way of addressing those so much older than yourself," added Emily.

Carly remembered with an uncomfortable sensation that the ghost had been about to explain something more to her when Mr. Nicholls appeared out of the fog. Perhaps if she and Maria had had more time, she wouldn't be getting so much "censure" right now.

"Well, I'm sorry," said Carly, looking around the table. "Maybe instead you can tell me where I can find a good novel to read tomorrow."

If anything, all the Brontës looked even more horrified.

"Read a novel? On a Sunday? Shocking!" said Mr. Brontë.

"Goodness, she really is a little savage!" said Branwell with a laugh.

Carly shot him a dirty look. What was wrong with this family? Every single thing she'd said at dinner had made them look at her like she was a lunatic. How had her simple plan of finding out more about them and getting her hands on a copy of *Jane Eyre* gone so wrong?

"Caroline, as tomorrow is Sunday, you will most certainly not need anything to read other than the Bible—a copy of which is in our room. As to your other comments, I believe you should spend the rest of the meal silently thinking about why they were wrong," said Charlotte.

"But—" started Carly.

"I said *silently*," reiterated Charlotte with a fierce look.

Carly subsided sulkily and spent the rest of the meal pushing pieces of turnip around her plate, wishing turnips did not grow so *very* well in Yorkshire, and thinking of ways to search the rest of the bookshelves in the house without getting into more trouble. She decided to ask nothing further until Monday, since the idea of reading a novel on Sunday seemed to horrify even people who wrote them.

In the meantime, Carly decided she would concentrate on Charlotte, Emily, and Anne. As instructed, Carly remained silent throughout dinner—although she was hardly thinking about her transgressions. More like "strategizing."

Mulling it over, she decided Anne would be the easiest to convince of her sincere desire to learn more about the family. *Ooh, I know what I'll do,* Carly thought. *I'll tell her it's because I miss my own family so much. Which is true, it's just not the family she thinks.* Emily she didn't hold out much hope for, unless she was somehow put in a mellower mood. And who could say what Charlotte would be like at any given moment these days?

Realizing it was too soon for a second attempt, Carly went up to bed as instructed and took one last look through the bookshelf before resigning herself to wait. It would be at least another day or two before she got home. Luckily, she was beginning to enjoy her adventure again, now that she *knew* how to get home, even if actually doing it was trickier than she'd expected. *At least now I know I'm not about to be murdered in my bed by an angry ghost*, she thought to herself.

In the morning, Charlotte's stern mood from the night before had not faded, so Carly made no mention of novels and tried to look pleased by the day's program: going to church, followed by reading aloud from the Bible and a cold luncheon at home. Then knitting or sewing for the poor until the light faded and it was time for dinner and bed.

Carly wondered how Mr. Brontë was going to give his sermon when he was almost blind. He must have committed everything he wanted to say to memory, she decided, because there was no squinting at anything or knocking papers off the pulpit. The church was cold, and Carly had a hard time not fidgeting. Some of the whiskers on the men and the bonnets worn by the women were startling, to say the least. Carly was pleased to notice Mr. Nicholls looking at them several times during the service.

"I think Mr. Nicholls likes your bonnet," she whispered to Charlotte at the end of a hymn.

"Hush!" admonished her governess, refusing to take the bait and look over at the curate.

Carly caught Mr. Nicholls eye and smiled brightly at him. She didn't want him to get discouraged. Mr. Nicholls pretended not to see Carly's smile and turned his eyes back to his prayer book. Carly almost forgot to kneel with the rest of the congregation because she was too busy envisioning Charlotte and Mr. Nicholls exchanging loving glances at church for the rest of their lives.

After lunch, they sat down to listen to Branwell read from the Bible. The previous Caroline, whomever she was, had been embroidering a piece of linen destined to be the cover of a decorative pillow. Charlotte told Carly she might work on it once she finished helping Anne wind some wool. Carly was dismayed to see that there was still a lot left to do, and no instructions for the pattern other than a rough pencil sketch.

"Please, I was hoping that one of you could teach me how to knit," she said, putting the embroidery back in the basket.

"Needlework is an important accomplishment for any young lady," said Charlotte, directing a quelling look at her troublesome charge.

"Of course, but as it's Sunday, I thought it might be nice to work on something to benefit others," said Carly. What she meant was, "I need to do something other than needlework because if I don't you'll wonder what happened to me when I make a complete mess of it."

"What an admirable sentiment," said Anne, smiling. "I think there can be no harm in teaching you to knit for the poor—as long as you don't neglect the more usual forms of needlework for a lady. If my sister does not mind."

"I suppose your mother will not object," said Charlotte.

"Oh, no," said Carly, thinking of her real mother. "My mom doesn't know how to knit, but she won't mind if I learn."

"Come sit with me by the window, Caroline," said Anne. "It is best to have good light so you can see the stitches. Very soon you will be able to do it without even looking at your work—until you need to turn a heel or something of that nature."

Carly was excited to learn how to knit—she'd been inspired the year before by reading *Rilla of Ingleside*, but since no one in her family knew how to knit and Carly didn't have any brothers at the front in World War One, her ambitions had come to nothing. Now that she'd seen the conditions of the poor in the village—the death of Bridget Martin still gnawed at her—she thought maybe helping make stockings for them would be a noble endeavor. *Although I'll bet my first try won't be anything the deserving poor would want to wear*, she thought.

The afternoon passed quickly—Anne gave Carly a stocking she had already knit an inch or two on to start with. "Beginning is always the worst part," she said. "It's much easier once you have something to hold onto."

Carly found what Anne told her to do quite difficult enough; she had no attention to spare to watch the time pass. Before she knew it, it was time for dinner and there were a couple of wobbly inches added to the beginning of the stocking. Anne tried to be encouraging, but Carly had the sneaking suspicion that as soon as she'd gone to bed Anne would rip it all out and re-knit it.

Only during dinner did Carly realize she hadn't had a chance to look for *Jane Eyre*. When tea was brought in, she excused herself and ran to Mr. Brontë's study. There was no fire, but she had brought a candle and scanned the titles on the shelves as quickly as she could. *Come on, come on,* she silently chanted. *Where can you be hiding?*

Finding nothing, she returned to the dining room to finish her tea. As she entered, she heard Charlotte say to Emily: "We can't possibly afford to have any new dresses this winter—I will turn our old ones if you can manage some of the preserves by yourself."

"I can help Emily finish the preserving and then help you with altering our dresses," said Anne.

"And they are not so very out of fashion," said Emily, a rare note of optimism in her voice. "The fabric you chose has worn well, I must say."

"I think our funds will stretch to some new ribbons, at least," said Charlotte, with the air of one comforting herself and others.

Carly took her seat silently, but her brain was working fast. She remembered Charlotte telling her how badly the sisters' book of poetry had done. Now they were talking about how they couldn't afford new dresses. Carly sipped some of her tea, not even noticing it had gone cold. She had been meaning to ask Charlotte for a copy of *Jane Eyre* as soon as they woke up on Monday morning, but now she had a better idea.

She didn't know how long it had taken *Jane Eyre* to become a bestseller, but it obviously hadn't happened yet if the Brontës couldn't afford new winter dresses. Charlotte had told Carly that her parents had left her some spending money for little items she might find she needed while they were away—new hair ribbons and the like. Larger purchases, like new dresses if Carly outgrew her current ones, were to be paid by her father's solicitor, a man who had been left in charge of their affairs while they were in India.

Charlotte hadn't told Carly the exact amount of her spending money, but Carly wondered if perhaps it was enough to purchase a book. *Wouldn't it be a nice surprise for Charlotte if I bought a copy of Jane Eyre? I don't know how much books cost, but she made it sound like my parents were pretty generous with my allowance.*

Thus Carly went to bed determined to accost Charlotte as soon as they woke up with a request for spending money. The picture of Charlotte's surprised delight when Carly showed off her purchase made Carly fall asleep with a smile on her face.

❧ CHAPTER TEN ❧

Awaking to find Charlotte already dressed and gone down-stairs, Carly scrambled into her dark blue dress and jumped down the stairs with a clatter. Emily sniffed disapprovingly, but even her superior grimaces had no power to dismay Carly this morning. She was ready to burst with all her good intentions for the day.

First she was going to get hold of her allowance. Then she was going to convince Anne to tell her all about herself and this Agnes Grey person—maybe it was Anne's best friend? Carly decided she should write a book someday entitled: "Francesca Erikson." If only Francesca were here to share the adventure! Then she'd have even better material.

Convincing Anne shouldn't be too hard, though, Carly thought. She just had to work up the appropriate expressions of contrition (for embarrassing the sisters last night at dinner), hopeful enquiry (to show how interesting she found the Brontës), and woeful anxiety about her parents (to tempt Anne to try and make her feel better).

Armed with the information she got from Anne, surely she could tempt Charlotte and even Emily to tell her their stories, too. Carly wished that Maria had been more specific about what sort of stories she needed, but maybe Maria herself would soon reappear and explain further? *I can ask her what a catharsis is, too—we were interrupted before she could explain,* Carly thought. *Never mind that I did the initial interrupting.*

So sure was she that her plan would work without a hitch that she ate two pieces of toast and drank a whole cup of tea before she turned to Charlotte.

"Miss Charlotte, may I please have some of my pocket money? I want to walk into the village before my afternoon lessons."

"I can't be spared to take you today. What do you need?" asked Charlotte.

Carly thought quickly. "I got my hair ribbon dirty when Mr. Nicholls almost ran me down with his horse, so I wanted to buy a new one. And a book." she added, as if in afterthought.

"What book?" asked Charlotte, looking up from the list of linens that needed mending.

"Oh, I don't know. I thought I'd look and see," said Carly, trying to sound nonchalant. "And the village isn't far—I'll be fine, really."

Both Charlotte and Carly were surprised when Mr. Brontë spoke.

"Nothing terrible can happen to the girl between here and the village," he said.

"Especially not to one so outspoken," muttered Emily with a hint of irony.

"Emily!" said Charlotte.

Emily sniffed. "She's too cheerful and frank."

Carly thought it time to turn the conversation away from her character and back to her proposed outing.

"I won't be gone long. Can you tell me where the bookshop is? And where I can buy a new hair ribbon?"

"The hair ribbon you can buy at the dressmaker's, which is next to Mr. Pottleton's book shop on the right after the inn. Father is right, I don't suppose you can come to much harm between here and Haworth," said Charlotte. "But I would prefer you go this morning; I think the weather may get worse as the day goes on."

"Thank you very much," said Carly, hastily swallowing her last mouthful of tea.

"The shops won't open for another half hour, so do your piano practice now," said Charlotte.

Some excitement left Carly, but even half an hour of piano practice couldn't dampen her enthusiasm for long. She bounded back up the stairs and plunked herself down on the seat.

"Please practice your scales!" Charlotte called after her.

Eager to keep Charlotte happy, Carly practiced her scales for a whole fifteen minutes before turning to Bach. In truth, the last five minutes might have been rather interrupted by glances at the clock, but she had concentrated remarkably well for the first twenty-five. When her time was up, she rushed to put on her coat and bonnet. Charlotte emerged from her father's study, smiling wryly at her.

"I thought a herd of wild horses was coming down the stairs. Please strive for a little more decorum, Caroline," she said, handing over a small purse. "Tuck this away out of sight, and don't linger too long in the book shop or the dressmaker's."

"No, I won't. I'll hurry right back!" said Carly with a big smile.

With that, she was out of the door and enjoying the autumn air.

The walk to the village was accomplished more quickly this time, because she was not carrying heavy baskets filled with spill-able things. She did, however, stop several times to hang over a gate and watch herds of sheep meander around their pastures. Carly walked in great good spirits, looking about, whistling, generally enjoying being by herself. Not only was it hard to sit still so much of each day, but Carly found it difficult to be around people all the time. Francesca loved it, but Carly preferred people in smaller doses. People always wanted to *talk* to you. And being left alone to practice the piano did not count, as far as she was concerned.

When she reached the village of Haworth she stopped first at the dressmaker's and purchased a hair ribbon of a pretty blue color. She took the precaution of inspecting the various coins in her purse before reaching the shop so she could count out the right number of shillings and pennies without hesitation. Tucking her purchase in her pocket, Carly went next door to the bookshop.

Before she went inside, she hesitated. It bore no resemblance to the bookshop that had gotten her into this mess, but she didn't want to stroll in and find herself in thirteenth-century China or, even more startling, twenty-ninth-century Morocco.

Seeing no alternative, she screwed up her courage and entered.

The shop was about the same size as the bookshop in Juneau, but much less cluttered. It was attended by one young man who looked up in surprise when Carly came in by herself.

"Can I help you, miss?" he asked politely.

Carly looked around. It would be fun to browse all the books, but she would not be so easily distracted from her quest. That was another thing Carly deplored in fairy tales—the hero getting so distracted by some unimportant detail that the whole thing turned into a disaster. She was not going to let that happen to *her*.

"Yes please, I would like to buy a copy of *Jane Eyre*," she said.

The young man looked puzzled.

"What is the title?" he asked.

"*Jane Eyre*. It's a novel by—" Carly stopped herself from saying "Charlotte Brontë" just in time. In the copy the old bookseller had showed her, the author's name was Currer Bell—just like on the book of poems.

"A novel by Currer Bell," she said.

"I don't think there is such a book," said the young man. "Are you sure you have the title right? Or the author?"

"Yes," said Carly, getting impatient. "It's called *Jane Eyre*, by Currer Bell."

"The only book I recall by Currer Bell was a volume of poems," the young man said. "But though the reviews were good enough, no one ever tried to buy a copy."

"Can I look in the fiction section and see?" Carly asked, trying to sound polite. *What if this silly young man has to order a copy for me? That could take weeks!* she thought with a shudder. *No, no. If he doesn't have it, I'll ask Charlotte for her copy. It would be nice to surprise her, but it'll be nicer to get home.*

"Look in the what?" the shopkeeper asked.

"The fiction section? You know, where you keep novels and stories."

"The few novels we have are on this shelf here," he said, leading her toward the back of the shop.

Carly stared at the tiny selection in dismay. Only one shelf of novels! Her thought that maybe the young man just didn't know he had a copy of *Jane Eyre* started to fade. Still, they both read through the titles. No *Jane Eyre* and nothing by Currer Bell.

Carly sighed in disappointment. She had so wanted to boost Charlotte's spirits. Oh, well—the important thing was not that she *buy* the book, but that she *read* it. Plenty of other people would buy it eventually. Right?

As she walked home, doubts plagued her. Charlotte had let her read the sisters' published book of poetry, but now Carly wondered with a sinking feeling if *Jane Eyre* hadn't been published yet. She ran over Maria's words, and found comfort in them: She had to read *Jane Eyre*, but she didn't have to read a published version.

Her mind relieved of one worry, Carly hurried on her way. The lane, which on her walk to the village had interested her with its hedges and grassy verge, had no power to distract her now. She wished Maria would reappear. Maybe she could let the ghost know she wanted to talk.

"Maria?" Carly called out tentatively. "Are you there? Can you hear me?"

Still walking, Carly looked around hopefully. Nothing disturbed the quiet of the lane except a sheep putting its head out through a gate and baaing at Carly.

"Quiet, you, you're not who I need to talk to at all!" she admonished. The sheep baaed again and went back to eating grass.

"Please, Maria. It's important. The bookshop didn't have a copy of *Jane Eyre*, and I messed up my first try at getting your sisters to tell me about themselves." Carly was starting to feel silly walking down a road talking to herself, but she persevered.

"What about their tales needs to be told? Are there specific things I should ask, or is any part of it good?"

Still no answer. Carly gave up and finished her walk back to the parsonage without further comments to or from the ghost. *What else can she have to do but try and help me? She even said no one else could see her*, Carly thought crossly.

As she walked up the steps of the parsonage, a new thought struck her. When she had snuck down the stairs that night, the sisters had been working on stories. Charlotte hadn't said the names of any of her characters, but maybe she was writing *Jane Eyre* this very moment! Carly decided to sneak a look at what they had been working on that night. She'd seen stacks of papers in the bureau in the dining room when Anne had opened it to retrieve an extra fork at dinner.

There was no time like the present. Carly opened the door quietly and slipped into the house. Without even pausing to take off her coat or bonnet, she went into the dining room. No one was there, and she ran to the bureau and opened the drawer

where she'd seen the papers. The handwriting was spidery and hard to read, but all she needed was a name she recognized.

She rifled through the first stack, skimming the words as fast as she could.

"Hmmm . . . hmmm . . . Heathcliff," she muttered to herself. "Nope, that's Emily's. Next pile. Nothing . . . nothing . . . Fiona! And Mr. Branchforth? No, this can't be it."

The only other set of papers was an assorted pile of sketches, notes, crossed-out plot ideas, and the like. Carly shut the drawer, frustrated. She would have to ask Charlotte, much as the idea made her nervous.

While she was still hanging up her coat, Charlotte came out of her father's study.

"I hope you had a pleasant walk. Did you find what you were looking for?"

"Not really," said Carly. "I got some ribbon, but I couldn't find the book. *Your* book."

"*My* book?" asked Charlotte in astonishment. "What book? I lent you a copy of our poems. Don't tell me you've ruined it somehow!"

"No, no. That's upstairs. I meant your novel. I wanted to buy a copy because you were so upset your poetry sold so few copies," said Carly, deciding that "so few" sounded better than "only two."

"I almost asked the bookseller to order me a copy," she continued. "But he was a very stupid man who hadn't even *heard* of your novel."

"Good heavens, what are you talking about?" said Charlotte, plainly astonished. "I don't have a novel!"

A horrifying premonition came to Carly—similar to the dark thoughts she'd had on the road, but worse, somehow.

"Haven't you . . . haven't you published a novel called—"
Charlotte cut her off.

"Certainly not. Are you telling me you walked into Mr. Pottleton's bookshop and asked for a novel written by Charlotte Brontë?" She sounded almost as horrified as Carly.

"No, I'm not *stupid*. I know you publish as Currer Bell," said Carly.

"I haven't published anything but that book of poems, and let me assure you that I have no intention of doing so!" said Charlotte emphatically.

"Okay, maybe not published . . . but have you *written* a novel?" asked Carly, her whole body starting to tremble. She could feel panic rising over her like a wave.

"I have some part of a story written, but I do not like it and I think I shall shortly burn it," said Charlotte.

"What's it about?" asked Carly, trying to stay calm.

"A beautiful and good heroine named Fiona Evelyn Burns, who is kidnapped by her wicked uncle for the sake of her fortune," said Charlotte.

"Oh, no," said Carly, ready to cry. "That's not the book I want. I want *Jane*—"

But again Charlotte interrupted her. "That is the only one, and I certainly will not let you read it, for it is terrible."

Carly's eyes smarted and her throat closed up. She desperately did not want to cry in front of Charlotte.

"Not even one other book?"

"No."

So it was true: *Jane Eyre* hadn't been written. There was no book for her to read.

She was trapped.

Carly's head started to spin. In agony, desperate to be by herself so she could cry, she rushed out the door into the garden. Her almost blind steps led her to the same bench where she had found Charlotte weeping; she stumbled over and sat down with her head in her hands. Sobs shook her whole body.

"It's not written! I'm trapped! What am I to *do*?" she choked out.

"Don't despair," came Maria's voice from beside her—although there was no visible sign of the ghost. "It is not written *yet*."

Her words had no power to comfort Carly. She'd been so sure she'd be home soon, so sure she knew how to fix everything.

And now! Now she was trapped. She didn't care if Charlotte or anyone else came out and saw her. She sat on the bench and cried as if her heart would break.

CHAPTER ELEVEN

It was at least a half hour before Carly could control her sobs. After she quieted down, she sat looking at her hands and tried to think. There was no *Jane Eyre*. So what was she to do? She couldn't stay here forever!

She remembered Maria's whispered words when she'd cast herself onto the bench: "It is not written *yet*." Carly seized on that "yet" like a life raft. *Yet.* Just because she couldn't get home right now didn't mean she was stuck with the Brontës forever. She would figure this out, and she *would* get home, even if she had to go on a hunger strike to force Charlotte to write.

Carly took a deep breath and tried to sort out her options. They weren't encouraging. She hadn't done even one of the things Maria said she needed to accomplish. *But*, thought Carly, *I'm not going to let that stop me from trying again. There must be a way home!*

Once she was over her shock, Carly was quick to make a new plan. If *Jane Eyre* hadn't been written, there was only one thing to do: make Charlotte start writing it as soon as possible.

As she rose to leave the garden, Maria appeared next to the bench, interrupting her solitude. The ghost stood, hands clasped demurely, looking at Carly.

"Good. You've gotten hold of yourself," she said dispassionately.

"No thanks to you! I think you might have warned me that *Jane Eyre* doesn't *exist* yet!" said Carly.

"I was going to, but we were interrupted," said Maria.

"And another thing," continued Carly, warming to her subject. "What do you mean I have to get your sisters to 'tell their stories'? To me? To anyone? What part of their stories? And how am I supposed to convince *Emily* that confiding in a twelve year old is a good idea? She totally hates me!"

"My sisters need to be freed from our past—it does not matter if you hear their story, but they must tell it, and the best way to do that is through *Jane Eyre*, *Wuthering Heights*, and *Agnes Grey*," said Maria. "The catharsis will be a difficult process to embrace. Our lives have not always been happy ones," she finished almost hesitantly.

"I kind of figured that—you *are* dead," said Carly.

Maria smiled briefly. "Yes. I am dead. But that does not mean I have stopped wanting to help my family."

"So let me make sure I have this straight. *Agnes Grey* is a book, too?"

Maria nodded.

"By Anne?" asked Carly, just to make sure.

Maria nodded again.

"And your sisters need to 'express themselves'—through their books—and I need to read *Jane Eyre* because that's what got me here."

"Yes, that about sums it up," said Maria.

"Except that expressing yourself doesn't seem like a popular pastime in this weird time period, and *Jane Eyre* doesn't exist," Carly said gloomily.

"But that is what suits you so particularly to this task!" Maria cried. "You are from a time when it *is* possible for a lady to 'express herself,' as you call it. Indeed, you seem very gifted in this area."

"Yeah, well, that doesn't help me when it comes to getting home, now, does it? I still need Charlotte to write a whole book!"

"You are resourceful. I am sure you'll figure something out," said the ghost in what Carly considered entirely too cheerful a tone.

"Hmph," was all Carly said in response, but she couldn't deny that she was feeling more hopeful. It was a relief to know she didn't have to get Emily or even Charlotte to fully open up to her. They just had to trust their stories to paper.

But, to Carly's mind, the most pressing problem was getting Charlotte to at least start *Jane Eyre*. She didn't care what Maria said: Writing a whole book would take some serious time. Best to get Charlotte started as soon as possible and worry about the rest later. Maria hadn't said that *Wuthering Heights* and *Agnes Grey* had to be finished for Carly to get home.

And that, Carly thought firmly, is my real mission. Determined, she stood and brushed off her skirts. Best to look as tidy as possible.

At that moment, Charlotte came out into the garden. She evidently felt that Carly had had more than enough time to recover from whatever had so upset her. Carly decided not to waste the opportunity—after all, there is no time like the present . . . *or the past,* thought Carly with an inward smile.

"Caroline, I do not understand that outburst, but I hope you have regained some measure of control over your feelings," Charlotte said, standing in front of Carly.

"Yes," said Carly, wishing her eyes weren't quite so red and stinging. "I was just thinking: You should write a different book. You should write a book that will make you feel better. I was upset because you're such a good writer, and you and your sisters have such a miserable time of it. If you would just write another book, I bet it would do a lot better than your book of poems."

Charlotte held up a hand to stop Carly.

"You will return with me to the house for lunch. I do not know where you get your outlandish ideas, but you will cease to express them."

Carly, by no means quelled, followed Charlotte to the dining room. Emily was sitting at the table, mending a tablecloth. Looking at Charlotte, Carly asked her, "Don't you *want* to feel better?"

"My feelings are of no concern to anyone but myself," said Charlotte stiffly, laying out silverware.

"A-ha!" said Carly. "That's where you're wrong! Lots of people care about your feelings—I do, your family does, Mr. Nicholls does—and if you wrote a book that also expresses how you feel, I'm sure you would be happier."

Charlotte stared at Carly in amazement.

"What in heaven's name are you talking about?" she asked.

Emily broke into the conversation. "Caroline, you seem to have the odd thought that the purpose of writing is to make one happy. Banish it. Writing exposes the charade that we call worldly happiness and the hypocrisy of those who claim to have it. It draws a portrait of our true natures and the mortal end we all must face."

It was Carly's turn to stare. What was Emily *talking* about? But she didn't want to put Emily any more out of humor than she normally was, so she nodded. "Right. If writing about charades makes you happy, that's great, too."

To her bewilderment, Emily glared at Carly and then turned back to her mending. Carly ignored this deliberate cold shoulder and returned her attention to Charlotte.

"Besides, you're right that what you're writing right now isn't very good. I looked."

Charlotte pinched her lips together as if to suppress a hasty retort. "You had no business reading my private papers."

"Fair enough," said Carly, keeping a wary eye on Charlotte—she had no desire to be slapped again. "But that doesn't mean I'm wrong. Do *you* think it's good?"

Charlotte frowned. "Its quality has nothing to do with your appalling behavior."

"I know I shouldn't have snooped into your personal things, but someone had to tell you! You said it yourself first, but you haven't done anything about it, have you?"

Emily gave a snort that sounded suspiciously like a laugh. "If you want to punish her, Charlotte, make her finish hemming the sheets Anne was working on yesterday. She has one of her headaches and it won't do Miss Impertinence here any harm to practice her needlework."

"What a good idea," said Charlotte. "Caroline, after lunch you will finish hemming the sheets, then you will make up your geography lesson in the evening instead of reading. Hopefully it will help teach you to mend your naughty ways."

"I don't know how to hem sheets. What is hemming, anyway?" asked Carly, forgetting for a moment the needlework skills of the other Caroline.

Emily raised her eyebrows. "Your education has been sadly neglected if you cannot perform so simple a task as hemming. How will you manage your own household one day?"

"To hem, you must finish the edges of the sheet by folding them over and sewing them in place so no threads can unravel," said Charlotte.

"Oh," said Carly, thinking this over. "That sounds dull."

"It is," agreed Charlotte. "That is why it is a suitable punishment."

Carly didn't have time to come up with a clever response, as the rest of the family entered the dining room for lunch at that moment. Carly liked the meal better than most of what the Brontës ate—the food served was so bland that Carly was sure Martha, the cook, had never heard of salt and pepper, much less garlic or herbs. Today, though, the leftover mutton from the day before had been chopped up and put into a dish with carrots and peas and thick brown gravy, all topped with thinly sliced potatoes. The flavors melted together and enhanced each other, which was a nice change from the excruciatingly plain food in previous meals.

After lunch, Carly was taken, along with what seemed like a *giant* basket of sheets, up to the schoolroom by Anne. Before Anne could leave her to her punishment, Carly spoke.

"I'm sorry you have a headache," she said.

"Thank you, Caroline. I expect I will feel better soon," said Anne, smiling kindly at Carly.

"Before you leave me with a million sheets to hem—"

"Only two," said Anne with another smile.

"You should know that unless someone shows me how to hem a sheet neither of them will get done," said Carly. "It's not like I can go look it up online here."

"What line?" asked Anne, confused.

"Oh. Ah, nothing," said Carly. A silly slip; it was 1846. Not only was there no such thing as the Internet, there was absolutely no point in trying to explain to Anne what the Internet was.

Anne sat down beside Carly and showed her how to hem the sheets, a task every bit as tedious as it sounded. Then Anne left, shaking her head at Carly's mother and previous governess. What had they been thinking to raise a girl so inept at needlework?

"I hope they don't mind sheets with blood speckles all over the edges," muttered Carly as she pricked her finger with the needle for the fifth time in as many minutes.

It was slow going. Carly kept pulling the thread out of the needle by accident and then struggling to get it back through the eye. The hem kept coming unfolded, or her pins would drop out. Once she finally got a section pinned up, her stitches were uneven and wobbly. After forty-five minutes of concentrated effort, Carly had about fifteen inches of hem done. She looked in despair at the sheet stretching out in front of her.

"Gahhhh! I'll never finish this," she said, throwing her hands up. "I'm sure I've been up here for hours and hours! They'll probably forget about me and I'll starve to death, and then I'll never get home, and some day, when they're looking for sheets, they'll come in and find my skeleton hunched with the rusty needle still in the cloth!"

(For the sake of drama, Carly decided to ignore the fact that she wasn't locked in, and all she had to do to prevent starvation was get up and walk downstairs.)

As she was enjoying the grisly thought of how her dried skeleton, hunched over its sewing, would forever remind the Brontë sisters of their cruelty, Anne opened the door.

"How are you getting along, Caroline? I've brought you a cup of tea and some bread with butter."

"Oh, thank goodness! I'm sure I would have starved to death if you hadn't remembered me!" said Carly, still caught up in her fantasy.

Anne laughed. "Surely that is a slight exaggeration. I hardly think Charlotte is the sort of governess who starves her pupils."

"It would be bad for business," agreed Carly. "She'd always have to be finding new students."

"Indeed," said Anne. "And you have no idea how difficult *that* can be. So you see, we are much more likely to feed you too much than too little."

"Of course, her next student would probably be better at needlework than me, so maybe she'll starve me to death and leave my corpse as a warning to other girls about the importance of learning to hem sheets," said Carly, surveying her handiwork.

Anne leaned over and looked at it too. She raised her eyebrows.

"I don't believe anyone would mistake you for a proficient needlewoman," she said. "Why haven't you learnt this? Your parents expect you to be proficient in all the domestic arts. Most girls learn to sew when they're five. You are already twelve."

"I don't know," said Carly. Silently, she thought to herself that it would have been nice of whatever or whomever had sent her back in time to have equipped her with the skills she would need so she didn't stand out so much. Surely if she could be transported through time, she could be endowed with the ability to sew. Or maybe sword fight. Sword fighting would be cool. Although there hadn't been much need for that yet.

Then she remembered that being whiny or ungrateful always got characters in books into trouble, like Eustace in *The Voyage of the Dawn Treader*, so she added aloud, "There are worse things than learning to hem sheets the hard way."

"And what is the hard way?" Anne asked.

"This," said Carly, showing off her battered fingers.

"Goodness, how many times did you poke yourself with the needle?"

"Too many to count," said Carly with a sigh. "I'll probably die of tetanus."

"Drink your tea, that will make you feel better," Anne said. "And then I will help you for a time. My headache is better and you obviously need the instruction."

"Thank you," said Carly gratefully.

True to her word, Anne helped her for almost an hour. Then she and Carly went downstairs to find Charlotte and report on Carly's progress. Watching how patient Anne was with her made Carly more determined than ever to help the sisters. She might not have read their novels, but living with the Brontës (and reading their poetry), had shown her how imaginative and clever they were. Anne in particular had been so kind. Carly didn't want them to live out their lives poor and miserable.

Inflicting unsolicited advice on people was more Francesca's thing than hers, however. Carly was happy to tell people how she thought they ought to be doing things, but she didn't do so uninvited, the way Francesca sometimes did. But since the Brontës showed no signs of asking her for advice, she would have to be brave. Hemming sheets was boring, but she was getting better at it. If Charlotte made her finish them because she was being impertinent, so be it. It was time for some straight-up twenty-first century common sense, Carly thought. Maria had told her that her willingness to express her feelings was what made her useful to the ghost in trying to free her sisters. It was time to follow up on her earlier attempt.

They found Charlotte in the kitchen with Emily, Tabby, and Martha making quince jam. With Mr. Brontë and Branwell away for a meeting in the village, the ladies of the house had decided to forego a regular dinner to give themselves time to process the pounds and pounds of fruit.

Before she could say anything, Carly was put to work cutting up quince. The fruit looked like a cross between a pear and an apple. As she chopped, Carly thought about how to start. The presence of Martha and Tabby made things harder. She knew from books and watching period dramas with her mom that talking about personal subjects in from of servants was frowned upon. But Tabby and Martha were practically part of the family and she had never noticed any of the Brontës censoring what they said in front of them. She bided her time, like a lion stalking a wildebeest, she thought, until there was a pause in the conversation.

"Miss Charlotte, I was thinking," Carly said. All eyes turned towards her.

"Oh, were you?" asked Charlotte politely, not pausing in her stirring of the first batch of jam.

"Yes. I was."

But before Carly could continue, Branwell burst into the kitchen.

"Where is Father?" exclaimed Charlotte, looking aghast.

"Oh, I left him with Mr. Nicholls," said Branwell. "But never mind that. I saw some fellows I know in the village and well, one thing led to another and . . ."

"Go on," said Emily in a hard voice—Carly couldn't blame her.

"The fact of the matter is, I need to borrow some money."

"Have you been drinking again?" asked Anne.

"Oh, Branwell, how much this time?" asked Charlotte.

"Ummm," said Branwell, leaning against the table and not looking particularly repentant.

"But we haven't any money!" exclaimed Emily. "At least, nothing except what we've put by to fix the roof!"

"Does Father know?" asked Anne.

"That's beside the point. I must pay my debts," said Branwell.

"Yes, *we* must," said Charlotte.

"And it is rather hard of you all to look so appalled when it is only a few pounds," said Branwell, staring sulkily around at everyone on the room.

Carly, already prepared to be brave, found herself quivering with anger. Branwell scared her, but they weren't alone on the stairs this time.

"What is *wrong* with you?!" she asked, throwing down the quince she held but keeping her knife.

Branwell looked over hazily, as if noticing her for the first time.

"I mean, seriously, what? What makes you think you can behave like this? All you ever do is whine to your sisters, and scare me, and act all paranoid. You're a jerk, and they need to realize that they *should* be angry," Carly continued, using her knife to gesture at the three sisters, all frozen in shock. "They *should* be mad at you for using the money to fix the roof to go out drinking with your friends. You are the worst brother ever. You treat them like they don't matter as much as you. Just because they're women doesn't mean you are worth more than them! They all do ten times the work you do, but you come in here and demand money—money probably saved from what *my* parents are paying Charlotte—like you're the king of England! You need to just stop it and they need to learn to express how angry they are. Otherwise you're all just going to stay miserable and poor and hating everything!"

Carly stopped, panting from her rant.

There was a dreadful silence. Tabby broke it, saying tartly:

"Mercy, what will the child say next? Not but what she has a point about you, Master Branwell!"

When Charlotte spoke, her voice was very quiet.

"I have spoken with you more than once today about your impertinence, Caroline. You have chosen not to listen. You will go upstairs and you will go to bed. You will not have any supper, and I expect to find you have mended your tongue before tomorrow. Do I make myself clear?"

"I think she needs a good beating," said Branwell, starting towards Carly.

"You will leave her alone. It is my place to decide her punishment. Go away and pay your debts," said Charlotte, restraining him with a hand.

Emily threw down the kitchen towel she held.

"I'll go with him to make sure he doesn't use it to buy more drink."

Branwell followed her out of the kitchen, protesting that if they didn't give Caroline a good hiding for her impudence they were failing in their Christian duty to root out sin.

Carly heard Emily snap back, "You're hardly one to lecture on the topic of sin, brother."

Carly carefully put the knife next to the leftover quince and wiped her hands. It wouldn't be very comfortable to go all night on an empty stomach. Charlotte pointed to the door. Carly walked up the stairs with lagging steps, trying to hear if anything was being said in the kitchen. But she could hear nothing.

Upstairs, Carly sat on the bed and considered the reaction she'd gotten. She wouldn't say it had gone *amazingly* well, but she hadn't been able to help herself when Branwell came in and started demanding money. Carly lay back spread-eagle on the bed and groaned artistically at the thought of waiting until morning for food. "Speak out on delicate subjects *after* eating" was definitely going on her list of lessons learned on this adventure.

To pass the time until she could fall asleep, Carly picked up the book of poetry. She made sure a pillow to hide it under was handy, because she was pretty sure that Charlotte's ban on reading for fun was still in place from that morning. She read until she heard someone coming up the stairs. The rumble of voices told her it was Mr. Brontë, back from the village, and Anne, helping him up the stairs. She listened to him go into his room and shut the door and Anne return downstairs. Carly continued reading, trying to ignore the gentle rumbles from her stomach.

Eventually it grew dark enough outside that Carly lit her bedside candle. The warm yellow light cheered her up so much that she forgot her hunger and the seemingly hopeless tasks standing between her and escape home. The flame stood up straight and proud until a draft from the window—which had an annoying habit of rattling in high winds, and there were *always* high winds on the edge of the moors—made it dance to the side. Carly watched a dribble of wax spill over the top and splash down the side of the candle into the china dish in which the candle stood.

When Carly had first arrived, she hadn't understood why the candles the Brontës used at night were in china saucers with handles— some even had little brass disks standing up from the handle. But soon she discovered that walking around with a candle made the wax spill much more; the china dishes caught it so it didn't splash on her hands or sleeve, and the brass disk reflected the light forward and out of her eyes. She thought that she'd suggest getting some to her parents when she got home—they would be so handy for when the power went out after a big Alaskan storm.

Concentrated as she was on the candle, it took a moment for Carly to hear the sound of footsteps below her. She listened hard. Yes! It was the light, steady tread of the sisters walking around and around the dining table—they must have finished the jam and they were working on their writing.

Determined to discover if her words had had any effect, Carly slipped off the bed and crept to the door. As she was about to turn the handle and sneak out onto the landing, she heard steps coming up the stairs again. The bed was too far to jump back in without making noise, so Carly stayed frozen, listening. It must have been Branwell; she heard the steps turn to the right at the top of the stairs and the door across from hers open and shut again.

Carly waited a minute or two more. No noise came from across the hall, so she slowly opened her door and peeked out. She definitely didn't want to run into Branwell tonight—he'd probably shove her down the stairs! The landing was deserted. She ducked out of her room and closed the door quietly behind her. Then she snuck downstairs—something she was getting good at—and crouched on the bottom step. She could peer through the railings at the dining room, but if one of the sisters happened to glance out into the dark hallway, it was unlikely they would see her behind the banister.

The door was only slightly ajar, so she couldn't see into the room the way she had last time, but she could hear well enough. The three sisters were in mid-discussion. Anne was saying, "Aunt Branwell did what she thought was her duty, but

I cannot think that we gave her as much difficulty as she always claimed."

"Nonsense," said Emily. "We were not particularly badly behaved. It was her own overly pious nature that made her treat us as she did."

"I for one will never forgive her for convincing Father to send us to that dreadful school," said Charlotte.

"And now Father says there is more typhoid in the village," said Emily.

Typhoid! thought Carly. *I hope it doesn't kill any more kids . . . or me.*

There was a short pause, then Anne's voice. "Perhaps Caroline was right, Charlotte. Perhaps you should abandon a project you find distasteful and write something else, something that gives voice to our experiences. Maybe we all should."

Emily gave a bitter laugh. "We tried to do that, remember? And remember how well our book of poetry sold?"

"There was nothing wrong with our poems. You know the reviews were complimentary. It was too difficult to intrigue a public that does not yet know our work. If we built up our pen-names . . ." Anne trailed off.

There was a longer pause. Carly held her breath, hoping that Charlotte wouldn't abandon the topic or decide to go to bed.

"I have always wanted to prove that a truly Christian heroine need be neither pretty nor charming to be compelling," said Charlotte, sounding thoughtful.

"Like us," said Emily. "I for one think it not a bad idea. I will let Cathy and Heathcliff show the full range of their emotions, to impress themselves upon the reader."

"Our lives have not been the happiest, it is true. Perhaps transposing that misery onto the pages of a novel would bring a measure of relief. That seemed to be what Caroline was suggesting," said Anne.

"It is an idea worth considering. Although what possessed Caroline to speak in that manner to Branwell, and to all of us, is beyond my understanding. She had best wake up tomorrow ready to apologize!" said Charlotte.

Carly had heard enough. Charlotte was thinking about her idea, and Carly thought her humble apology the next morning would go much better if she wasn't found eavesdropping tonight.

She crept carefully back upstairs, thrilled to the bone with excitement. Charlotte was seriously thinking about writing another book—a book that *had* to be *Jane Eyre*!

As she lay with her eyes closed, Carly thought of all the ways she could suggest to Charlotte that the heroine of her new book be called "Jane."

Subtly, of course, she thought, drifting towards sleep. *I'll have to be subtle about it.*

∾ CHAPTER TWELVE ∾

Carly woke herself up in the morning muttering: "Mushroom and sausage pizza with extra cheese . . . blueberry sourdough pancakes with real maple syrup . . . venison stew and Dad's fresh baked bread . . ."

Her rumbling stomach deserved full credit. Tabby could probably hear it downstairs in the kitchen! Beside her, Charlotte was still asleep.

Carly got out of bed and dressed quietly. Then she sat down on the straight-back chair and waited for Charlotte to wake up. She spent the time trying to arrange her face into what she intended as a chastened but hopeful look. Or maybe she should start with chastened and add hopeful partway through her apology?

Regardless, her humble apology would go over better before she got food. The pangs of hunger would make her look more woeful and make Charlotte more inclined to forget her anger of the previous night.

Eventually Carly got tired of waiting and kicked the leg of the chair a few times to make some noise—then stopped as Charlotte stirred. Carly put on her best "I'm sorry" face. Taking a deep breath, she began her carefully composed speech.

"I hope you slept well, Miss Charlotte," Carly paused and clasped her hands in her lap. "I want to offer you my deepest, most sincere, most *humble* apology for last night. That I, your pupil, could so misbehave fills me with grief . . ." Carly had much more like this all ready to spout off—she was kind of enjoying the pathos. If she had to apologize, then she might as well do a first-rate job.

Unfortunately for the drama of the moment, Charlotte broke in to say:

"Yes, I certainly hope you are sorry. It was shocking behavior—your parents would not be at all pleased to hear of your conduct."

"No, they would be very disappointed in me," said Carly, not hesitating to put words in the mouths of her unknown parents.

"You will also offer your apologies to my brother," continued Charlotte—who ruined the stern tone by adding to herself, "Though he really is the most aggravating creature sometimes."

Carly kept quiet, correctly assuming that Charlotte wanted no further comment from her on the subject.

After Charlotte dressed, she accompanied Carly downstairs, where Carly offered a less ornate apology to Branwell—and hoped Charlotte couldn't tell she didn't mean a word of it. Realizing that books cannot be written overnight, no matter how much she might want them to be, Carly decided it would be a good idea to give Charlotte a couple of days to work on *Jane Eyre* before she started hinting that faster was better. She didn't want to interrupt the creative process too much.

Besides, she thought as she munched a piece of cold toast spread with marmalade, *I'd better give her a day or two to forget I'm in disgrace. Dang, that'll mean looking all keen to do lessons . . . and I'll have to finish hemming that sheet.*

Carly's lack of ability with a needle had so shocked all three sisters that Carly was being made to finish the two sheets as practice. Thinking about the "treat" in store for her, Carly ate her toast as slowly as possible, taking small bites and chewing each one methodically. She was dipping a plain piece of toast into her tea when Charlotte called her to order.

"Caroline, please finish so we may begin catching up on your lessons."

Carly gulped down the last of the tea and crammed the toast in after it. It was going to be a long couple of days.

"I'm ready," she mumbled.

"Don't talk with your mouth full, please," said Charlotte, leading the way up to the school room. There, she picked up the French grammar and looked at it grimly.

So did Carly.

"I hate doing things I'm not good at, especially when they don't *mean* anything," Carly blurted out, thinking of the endless grammatical rules in the pages before her.

"A very natural feeling," Charlotte said. "That does not mean, however, that you will be allowed to shirk your lessons. If I must teach, you must learn."

"How about instead of teaching me French today, you write and I read one of your dad's books on botany?"

Charlotte was about to reject Carly's suggestion out of hand, but paused, an arrested look on her face. "Let us compromise. I will fetch a book on botany—" Carly sat up straighter in delight, "that I purchased in Belgium."

"So it's in French," said Carly, slumping back down.

Charlotte ignored this interruption. "I will pick out the simpler sentences and we will parse them together. You are quick enough in the other subjects that while I would rather be writing, I find teaching you is not the agony it so often is."

Carly smiled to herself. She knew that was Charlotte's version of a compliment.

Without waiting for a reply, Charlotte left the room and returned with a fat brown volume entitled *Alphabet Flore*, by Pierre-Joseph Redouté. She turned over the pages until she came to a sentence involving roses.

"You see, Caroline, the verb must agree in person and number with the subject of the sentence. What would happen if there were more than one rose?"

"The verb would need to be third person plural," said Carly.

"And how do you form the third person plural of *avoir*?" asked Charlotte.

She and Charlotte held the *Alphabet Flore* and the French grammar open and Carly wrote out each sentence on her slate. After she had correctly identified all the parts of the sentence and translated it (with help from Charlotte on the more difficult words), she rewrote it using a different subject, verb, or tense.

She kept waiting for the familiar panic to set in, but between her interest in the botany and Charlotte's aid in understanding both the mechanics of a sentence and the reasons behind them, Carly did not feel the numbing panic that had always before made her mind go blank when she tried to read French. *If this keeps up I'll have no excuse not to apply to that camp Grandmother and Francesca are so keen on*, she thought to herself. She'd ridden a horse (with Mr. Nicholls in charge of the steering of it, but still), and here she was making real progress on a foreign language! Now able to see concrete examples of the grammar she was trying to learn, the time passed faster than Carly had expected.

For the next few days, she focused on her lessons and on various household management skills that Emily thought she ought to know (like how many pints of marmalade were needed to get a family of five through the year—a lot more than Carly would have guessed). In the evenings, Anne helped her with needlework while Charlotte read aloud. Interspersed were excursions to the village, a drawing lesson in the garden, and a short walk on the moors, where they met with Mr. Nicholls, who walked them back to the parsonage. Carly tried to dawdle so he and Charlotte would have time to talk in relative privacy. Mr. Nicholls pleased Carly by bowing to her exactly as he did to Charlotte—making her feel very grown up—but his attention was clearly on her governess. Carly watched with satisfaction as Mr. Nicholls shortened his stride to match Charlotte's, bent his head to catch her every word, and offered his arm to help her over a rough patch of ground.

Each night after she was sent to bed, Carly listened for footsteps in the room below. Each night she fell asleep, reassured by the light tread that writing progress was being made.

On the evening of the third day—a Thursday—Charlotte beckoned Carly over to where she sat embroidering a handkerchief for her father.

"Caroline, I am most pleased with your progress this week," she said with an approving nod. "Your French verbs in particular are benefitting from your diligent study."

Carly was pleased Charlotte had noticed. Foreign languages would always be a struggle, but one-on-one tutoring by a patient Charlotte combined with a lack of distractions (although Carly wouldn't have minded a *few* of the distraction modern life offered . . . like her friends or cross-country practice, for example), meant that Carly could now conjugate at least the most important verbs without panic setting in and making her forget what little she knew. *I wish it took less effort though*, she grumbled to herself.

Carly went to bed, her spirits high from the thaw in Charlotte's attitude, and already plotting how to get a peek at Charlotte's work, just to double check it was *Jane Eyre*. She jumped up from the bed, ready to start the day. Charlotte had already gone downstairs, but Carly's clothes were laid out as usual on a chair. She hurried into them, glad to have a plan. Even buttoning all the buttons up on her dress didn't seem tedious.

When she reached the dining room, Carly realized she'd slept later than she'd thought: Of the family members, only Charlotte and Branwell remained. Branwell looked pale and haggard, and he winced when Carly clattered her teacup in its saucer.

"Shh!" he said, holding his head in his hands like it might break.

"What?" asked Carly, taking malicious pleasure in speaking louder than usual. Branwell groaned.

"Good morning, Caroline," Charlotte said, ignoring her brother. "We will begin our lessons today with drawing in the garden. I want you to study how the morning light creates a different effect from the afternoon light, and to attempt to capture on paper the passion nature provokes."

"Okay!" Carly said, loudly enough to make Branwell groan again.

"Take her away and beat some sense into her," Branwell muttered. "Maybe it will make her better at French."

"Branwell, be quiet this instant!" said Charlotte. "How dare you say such rude things to *my* pupil?"

Did the whole family laugh at her behind her back for how hard she had to work at French and German? Carly wondered miserably. She wanted to get away from Branwell as fast as she could, but Charlotte put a restraining hand on her arm.

"Do not mind him, Caroline," said Charlotte loudly. "He is in a bad temper because he overindulged last night. He only wants someone else to feel as miserable as he."

With that parting shot, she walked Carly out and slammed the dining room door. Another groan sounded through the wall.

But even Charlotte's spirited defense couldn't make Carly un-hear Branwell's words. All her pleasure at her progress evaporated. What was the point of trying so hard if people were just going to make fun of her anyway? Carly hated to be bad at things, and the fact that most of school came naturally to her meant that she was particularly sensitive to criticism about foreign languages. Even though she knew Branwell was a jerk, it still hurt.

As a distraction, Carly threw herself into drawing a quince tree in the garden. By the time she was finished, her fingers were stiff and her back ached from hunching over her paper. She stretched gratefully and considered her efforts. Not as bad as she'd thought it would be. She followed Charlotte inside and spent the remaining time before lunch pretending to memorize German verbs—but Branwell's words from breakfast caused all her old insecurities to come flooding back, and she stumbled through words that she had known yesterday. Charlotte was especially gentle in her manner, having no doubts as to the cause of Carly's nerves.

Lunch involved too much cabbage, making Carly think longingly of grilled cheese with tomato soup—and home. To make matters worse, Emily was in a sour mood. Apparently the butcher was trying to over-charge her for the mutton she'd ordered. Emily took out her temper on a still haggard Branwell, sniping at him on the subject of Christian behavior until Carly thought she'd scream. Finally Mr. Brontë put an end to the squabble.

"Forgiveness is a virtue we all must practice. I have forgiven my son for his reckless behavior, so let us hear no more about it."

Carly raised her eyebrows at the same time Emily did.

Charlotte saw them both, and hastily said, "The duty of any Christian must be to follow where God leads us. I just started—I mean, heard a story of a young woman—Jane, I believe her name was—whose frail human heart wanted that which was not possible, whose every feeling revolted against answering God's call. But once she died to self she heeded His will and shall travel to India to aid her husband in spreading God's word."

Carly stopped pushing peas around her plate and felt a thrill of excitement. Proof! Here was proof that Charlotte was writing *Jane Eyre*! She was so happy that even the memorization of dates in English history after lunch didn't seem tedious.

Charlotte had left her to write out a list of key events during Elizabeth's reign when Maria appeared, interrupting Carly's cheerful humming as she scribbled the dates down.

"What are you doing here?" asked Carly in a hushed tone.

"I wanted to tell you that you are making progress—but there is more."

"*More*?!" said Carly with dismay. "What kind of more?"

"Charlotte has started work on *Jane Eyre*, but you must make her see that convention cannot stop her from writing what is in her heart—*everything* that is in her heart. The way she is writing it now . . . I fear it is not good enough."

"Maria, she's writing *Jane Eyre*! She even talked about it at lunch! What more do you want from me?" Carly cried.

"But she is not!" Maria whispered impatiently.

Carly stared at her in disbelief.

"What, is she writing *Jane Pear* or something?"

"No! Charlotte has got the name right. It is the *feelings*! You heard her yourself—she is planning to have Jane be a proper Christian heroine who sails to India to do missionary work!"

"So?" said Carly, not understanding Maria's agitation.

"She is following convention, not being true to her character or herself. It must be everything in her heart, or it is all for naught!"

Carly groaned. "How am I supposed to help her with that? How do I make her?"

"You must!" said Maria urgently—and disappeared. Carly heard footsteps on the stairs and straightened up in her seat.

"Ugh, I'll try, but a hint about *how* would have been nice!" she whispered toward the ceiling.

Charlotte looked into the room.

"I thought I heard voices," said Charlotte, looking around the school room.

"Just me," said Carly.

Charlotte nodded pointedly at Carly's slate and then went back downstairs. Carly returned to her work with a sigh, her earlier cheer gone. All she could think about was how to follow Maria's newest instructions. It would be horrible if Charlotte wrote the wrong version of *Jane Eyre* and Carly never got home. What would she *do*?

∽ CHAPTER THIRTEEN ∽

When Carly came down the stairs the next morning, her head felt heavy and she had a nagging headache behind her eyes. She had tossed and turned the night before, unable to get comfortable. She didn't know how to make Charlotte—or Anne or Emily—stop being so *proper* and use the talent they clearly possessed, and all she really wanted at this point was to go home. Dresses with full skirts and candles lighting the way to bed and servants bringing you fresh baked bread in the mornings were all very well and good, but Carly missed her family, her house, her *time*. Nineteenth-century England was way better on paper than in real life—the fetid grave water supplying the village being number one on Carly's list of things she wouldn't miss.

When she had finally fallen asleep the night before, she had dreamed of poor Bridget Martin. She woke up feeling worse than ever. Carly did not belong here. Her failed attempts to show the Brontë sisters what they needed for their own happiness (and Carly's freedom) only made her feel worse and worse. She tried giving herself a stern talking-to as she dressed, but her stiff upper lip insisted on quivering, and she could not help wishing that someone else had been chosen to help the Brontës out of this mess.

But no. Carly took a deep breath. She might wish someone else had been sent to Haworth Parsonage, but the fact remained: She was the one stuck here. Her desperation expressed itself as a newly firm resolve to *make* Charlotte see that she could not hold back while writing *Jane Eyre*. Not only was she homesick and tired, but Carly was beginning to get fed up with the sisters' apparent determination to accept their lives as they were—no matter how miserable.

Carly raised her head, straightened her shoulders, and marched into the dining room. Charlotte was waiting for her; the rest of the family was finishing breakfast. Carly, remembering past attempts to lecture Charlotte, prudently loaded her plate up and got a cup of tea *before* she spoke. But as soon as she had a substantial meal on her plate, she went straight to the point.

"Miss Charlotte, I was thinking," she started.

"Oh, lovely," muttered Emily.

"It's about your writing."

Charlotte stiffened. "I believe we have established by now that my writing is none of your concern."

"This pupil of yours is remarkably outspoken," said Mr. Brontë in disapproving tones. "Can you send her home?"

"Unfortunately, her parents are in India. I can scarcely send a child home to a house that has been shut up," said Charlotte.

"Perhaps you ought to beat her more frequently. It might improve her character," he said.

Carly tried to ignore her headache—and Mr. Brontë's scary words—and keep focused on what Charlotte needed to understand.

"I think hemming sheets is worse than being beaten, so I bet my character is already improved. But that's not the point. The point is that Miss Charlotte needs to write what is in her heart. It's not like she enjoys teaching."

This statement produced silence around the table. Why did the whole family have to stare at her like she was nuts all the time? Carly wondered.

"You have to be brave—like ripping off a Band-Aid. Just . . . go for it." Carly stopped short and took a deep breath, trying to hold back a further torrent of nervous words.

Charlotte stood. "I have no notion of what a 'Band-Aid' is, but let me be clear: You do not seem to understand, no matter how many times I tell you, Caroline, that you are being interfering and impolite. You will stop, or I *will* be forced to whip you. Your hands look sore enough from your attempts at sewing; I don't think my hitting them with a ruler would be a pleasant experience. But rest assured, I will certainly do so if you do not learn to control your tongue."

"I *know* I'm being interfering!" cried Carly. "That's my *job*! I have to make you see! Do you like living *like* this, never saying what you feel? Always keeping silent? You—all of you—are so talented. I can see that and I haven't even read your books yet. But you're *wasting* it! Why won't you *do* something?"

"I hardly think that the opinion of a young girl is one by which I will be guided," said Charlotte. "You have no reason to be concerned with my affairs—I have no need of your assistance, and yet you persist in pushing yourself forward."

Carly stood up, too, bracing herself against the table and staring Charlotte in the eyes. "No, you don't understand. Why won't you *listen*? That's the whole problem."

Branwell chose this moment to look up from his eggs.

"Goodness, listen to the little lunatic ranting at you. Have you always been this peculiar, girl?"

This was the last straw.

"I'm trapped here! If you don't do this, I'm trapped forever!" Carly screamed.

With that, she turned and ran from the room, leaving her breakfast untouched. She needed to get out, out of this house, away from everyone. Carly dashed an angry tear off her cheek and stood in the middle of the hall, thinking furiously. She'd go for a walk. All their walks over the last few days had been boringly short, but she could ask Tabby for a snack and take herself out for a real walk.

Decided, Carly ran back to the kitchen.

"May I have some bread and cheese and an apple?" she asked Tabby as calmly as she could. "I'm going out."

"What you be needing with more food when you've just had your breakfast?" grumbled Tabby, even as she started to slice the bread.

"It's for later," said Carly.

"Hmph," was all Tabby replied. But Carly noticed she cut the slices of bread nice and thick and put in a big piece of cheese and *two* apples.

"Thank you very much," said Carly, wrapping it all up in a napkin.

"You're not going to have much time for your walk with the weather bidding to get nasty," Tabby called after her.

Carly brushed off Tabby's words; she had to be alone, *away*, or she was going to explode. Because she was trying to sneak out, she didn't slam the front door, even though she wanted to. She did take some satisfaction in stomping all the way around the house and through the garden. The stomping helped her calm down, but she didn't slow her pace until she was well out of sight of the house. If they couldn't see her, they couldn't call her back.

Despite how badly her attempts to reach Charlotte were going, Carly's heart lifted as soon as she stepped out of the trees onto the moor. She was still upset, trapped, and homesick, but out here it was easier to bear. It still mattered—she wanted so desperately to succeed at this adventure and to get home—but at least now she didn't feel like she was confined in a cage. Her headache even receded as she strode along the winding track.

The day was overcast and the breeze sharp enough that Carly walked faster and faster to keep warm. On and on she went, swinging the napkin with her snack tied in it and trying not to think about anything at all. She was tired of thinking and thinking and thinking. Thinking had gotten her nowhere. She'd been so pleased when Charlotte had started writing *Jane Eyre*. Then Maria's claim that just writing it wasn't good enough . . .

Carly shook her head to clear the thought away. She'd look at the moor. Look at each clump of heather or broom or gorse and see if she could spot a grouse—or an adder, although it was probably too cold for them to be out.

Today the lonely landscape suited her mood perfectly; she reveled in the odd mixture of long vistas and sudden hidden valleys. Carly wished she'd been able to see the moors in summer when the heather was in full bloom. *It must smell great*, she thought. *But please, please don't let me still be here when next summer comes.*

She felt her head start to ache with renewed intensity and her eyes grew hot, so she walked even faster and tried not to think about the future.

It didn't take Carly long to get further along the path than she'd ever been. She didn't meet anyone as she walked—once in the distance, she saw what could have been Mr. Nicholls riding, but the horseman was so far away she couldn't be sure.

The further and longer she walked, the better she felt. After a time, Carly realized that she wasn't horribly upset any more. The idea of returning to the house crossed her mind, but it immediately made her feel worse, so she kept her face turned away from the parsonage and into the fresh air of the moor. Stopping for a moment, she extracted one of the apples from her bundle and resumed walking, happily munching.

When she'd finished the apple, she hid the core under a gorse bush and licked her fingers clean. None of the scenery was familiar, but she was still on the beaten track. There was an ominous black cloud behind her, though. It didn't look like it was raining . . . yet.

Carly sighed. She didn't want to turn back. She wanted to stay out all day and ignore everything she had to do. Even the weather was trying to thwart her, she thought, looking rebelliously at the cloud.

I don't care; I'm going to eat my bread and cheese, and then I'll start back. Carly found a rock to sit on, faced resolutely away from the approaching cloud and the chilly breeze, and opened her napkin bundle. When she was done, she stood up and turned to look at the path home.

No, not home, she corrected herself. *Just a house.*

The black cloud had gotten closer and the wind was colder than she'd expected after sitting with her back to it. Carly wasn't stupid, and having grown up in a place where not taking bad weather seriously could kill you, she knew that it had been foolish to delay her return to the parsonage. *I'll run,* she thought. *It doesn't look so bad, and probably the worst that will happen is I get wet.*

She started to run back along the path, but realized quickly that it was too rough to be safe. Her grandfather always said, if you want to break your leg, run through the woods. Carly thought that the moors were another good spot. So even though the cloud was right in front of her and the day had gotten as dark as twilight, Carly slowed to a fast walk.

Before she had gone fifty yards the cloud opened up and started dumping rain. It came down so hard that Carly was instantly soaked to the skin, her hair plastered to her head. The rain hissed into the gorse and heather beside the path and formed puddles along the track. Carly put her arms up over her head to shield her face and kept going. It was raining so hard that she couldn't see further than fifteen feet in any direction. And it was *cold*.

Doggedly she kept to the track, no longer almost running, but hurrying as well as the wet and slippery ground would allow. She was feeling colder by the minute, and the rain continued to beat down. Once or twice, she tried looking around, but could see nothing beyond the moor immediately next to her on either side. The horizon was shut off and any landmarks were lost in the pelting rain.

Carly started to shiver. She felt stupid for ignoring the threatening cloud—she knew better, she really did. In Juneau, a whole week of school each year was devoted to survival skills, and just because she was upset, she'd forgotten everything she knew. Well, she was going to do her best not to make any more mistakes today.

After twenty minutes, the rain stopped pelting down and began falling hard and steadily. Carly could see a little further into the distance, and searched eagerly for a landmark she recognized. Much to her dismay, she saw fog creeping up the hillside below her.

"Rain *and* fog? That isn't fair," she said out loud. But pointing out that it was unfair did nothing to stop the fog, and soon Carly was shivering harder. The fog brought with it more bitter cold, and Carly wrapped her arms around herself as she stumbled along the now-flooded path. Her head was starting to ache so badly that she couldn't do more than focus on putting one foot in front of the other and staying on the track.

Suddenly she fell over the bank of a tiny stream swollen by the rain, which the path crossed, soaking her feet and ankles. Carly stood shaking in the rain and mist, terror fighting to rise up in her throat. She had not crossed a stream on her walk out.

She peered around, trying to see anything that would tell her where she was. The rain and fog were too heavy. If only her head didn't ache so, she would be able to figure out what to do. *Think!* she told herself. *Where can you be? Is there any ditch the path crossed that might become a stream after this much rain?*

But she knew there wasn't.

"I'm lost," she said out loud, testing the words to see if they could be true. "I'm lost," she repeated. "I'm lost!" she yelled as loudly as she could. Yelling made her head hurt, so she stopped. She was obviously on the wrong path, but she had always been on a path and had never walked across open moorland, so this trail must meet up with the main track at some point.

But when you were lost, the best way to be found was to stay where you were.

Carly stood, hesitating. The cold finally decided her, and she turned around and walked back up the path away from the stream. She didn't know if more than one track met this one, so she decided to stop at the first junction and hope it was where this track met the trail home. Then she'd wait until the rain and fog lifted enough to see if she was going in the right direction. Carly walked slowly, peering through the still heavy rain. She should have noticed much earlier that this track was too narrow and twisty to be the main one, but she was cold and tired and she hadn't. How far had she come in the wrong direction? She had no idea.

Finally, stumbling because she was so cold and wet, Carly found a point at which another path crossed the track. But until she could see further, she couldn't tell if this was the trail she'd come from. She knew it would be supremely stupid to pick a random direction and hope—she could go the wrong way for miles before she knew her mistake, and she had seen no sign of shelter further out on the moors. So she did the only thing she could: she stayed where she was and waited for the rain and fog to clear.

To keep herself company, she started reasoning through everything out loud.

"I left during breakfast, so I don't need to worry about being stuck out here all night—the weather will lift before that," she said to herself.

"It was stupid not to go back as soon as you saw that cloud," Herself replied.

"Yes. That was pretty dumb. But I couldn't stand the thought of being shut inside with all of *them*. And my head still hurt. A lot."

"Best thing to do is huddle together for warmth, since I can't get dry," she muttered to herself.

"Who are you planning to huddle together with?"

Sitting down on a rock, Carly drew her knees up to her chest and hugged them. She had to conserve body heat. If she got too cold, she would walk in a circle around the rock until she warmed up—no chance of losing her way if she kept it in sight the whole time. She wished she had a thermos of hot cocoa or tea. Not that there were thermoses in 1846, but Carly figured that as long as she was wishing for impossible things she might as well wish for something good. Like hot cocoa. With whipped cream and chocolate sprinkles. And maybe a fresh baked cookie. Yes, definitely a fresh chocolate chip cookie, warm and gooey from the oven. And some rain gear. And Francesca to keep her company. This was the least tickety-boo situation Carly had ever been in and she wanted her best friend.

Thinking of her best friend made Carly remember how she'd brushed Francesca off when Francesca urged her to apply to French camp.

"If I get home alive," Carly mumbled to herself, her chattering teeth making it hard to talk. "*If* I get home alive I will send in that application *so fast*. It can't be worse than this. Adventures aren't supposed to be life-or-death, they're just supposed to *seem* like it."

She was starting to sound hysterical, even in her own mind. Carly tied the wet napkin that had held her bread, cheese, and apples over her head. It was as wet as her hair, but it would help keep some of her body heat from escaping. Carly had heard somewhere that a person lost almost half of his or her body heat through the head, and she didn't have anything else to use as a hat. She unfolded her legs stiffly and stood up to walk around in a circle, always keeping the rock and path in sight. She swung her arms vigorously and hopped up and down. She could feel her blood flowing and kept at it until she was out of breath. Then she sat back down and curled up again.

Carly wasn't sure how many times she repeated this pattern. It felt like she'd been doing it her whole life—that there was nothing in the world but cold rain and fog and a small rock that she sat on until she was too cold and then a wet path and wet heather that she hopped up and down on until she could feel her fingers and toes again. Always she was looking outwards, trying to see if the rain or fog was lifting. But nothing changed, and Carly knew that she was getting dangerously cold.

She stopped sitting on the rock and instead walked slowly around and around it, still swinging her arms.

"I have to stay warm. I have to wait until I can see to try and get back. Or so someone can find me. I'm on a path," she repeated to herself. "I have to wait here, and stay warm."

Her head hurt so much. Would it be all right to sit down on her rock again for a minute? Carly plodded in a circle a few more times, trying to decide how cold she was.

"Just for a minute. One minute," she said, sinking onto the rock and pulling her legs up to her chest. Gingerly, she rested her aching head on her knees.

"I know I need to keep moving, but I'll rest until my head hurts less," she murmured to herself.

She meant to get up in a few seconds. She meant to keep walking in a circle and swinging her arms because she knew she had to stay active and warm. She knew that to give in to the cold was a mistake, but her head hurt so much . . .

"I'm an Alaskan, and we know how to survive," she muttered to herself.

But she did not get back up. The rain poured down and Carly sat, as still as a statue on the rock. She did not lift her head to see if the fog had lifted. She did not rub her hands together or wiggle her toes to keep up her circulation. She drifted near to sleep. She shivered, and her head felt hot even though she was cold.

Once she tried to lift her head, but she could not. Instead she lay on her side on the rock with her knees still drawn up to her chest. And she did not move.

⤙ CHAPTER FOURTEEN ⤚

Hours went by. The rain lessened and the fog drifted away. Still Carly did not move. Through the patter of the rain on the moor, the sound of hooves echoed sharply. All of a sudden there was a shout.

"She's here! I've found her!"

Mr. Nicholls reined in his horse and leapt down. He put his hand on Carly's shoulder.

"Caroline, can you hear me? Are you awake?"

Another horse—a stout farm horse borrowed from a local farmer bearing Branwell—stopped next to him. Branwell dismounted and looked at Carly.

"Is she alive? I'd never forgive myself if . . ." he trailed off, twisting his hat in his hands.

"It's cruel weather for a child to be out in," said Mr. Nicholls, shooting Branwell a glance of disgust for his handwringing after the fact.

Carly moaned and tried to sit up.

Mr. Nicholls picked her up in his arms and said over his shoulder, "Quick, Branwell, fetch me two of the blankets in my saddle bags. She's almost frozen. I need to get her wrapped in something drier before we ride home."

Carly couldn't say anything. Her head was whirling and she wasn't sure what was happening. Mr. Nicholls was there, she could tell that, and he seemed very worried about someone. She tried to tell him that he shouldn't worry; she knew all sorts of survival skills. Who was it they were trying to dry off? How silly of that person to get so wet and cold that they needed rescuing by Mr. Nicholls.

"Ow," she muttered in faint protest as Mr. Nicholls ruthlessly dried her with one blanket and wrapped her securely in the other.

"Hold on to her while I mount. Then hand her up to me," he commanded.

Carly was held across his saddle brow, too dazed to be nervous about riding, as Mr. Nicholls started back towards the parsonage, not even waiting for Branwell to mount and follow. The rain continued to drizzle down, but the thick wool blanket covered most of Carly. The motion of the horse made her dizzier than ever and she closed her eyes to try and still her spinning head. She slipped out of consciousness again—not really asleep, not really awake, but trapped in her spinning head by how cold she was.

As they neared the parsonage, Mr. Nicholls shouted again, jolting Carly out of her stupor.

"Miss Emily—I've found her! Call back the others."

"Thank God," said Emily. "I feared she had fallen and broken her neck!"

Without waiting to hear the rest of her sentence, Mr. Nicholls rode on to the house. When he arrived he gave another shout and Anne rushed outside.

"Oh, thank goodness! Where was she? Bring her inside—we've summoned the doctor; he should be here soon," said Anne all in one breath.

"Let me hand her down to you. Can you support her weight while I dismount?" asked Mr. Nicholls.

"Yes, yes of course," said Anne, reaching up.

Carly was unable to help them—and indeed, she struggled to understand who they could be talking about. Not her, surely? She'd just gone for a walk. Going for a walk didn't mean one had to call the doctor!

But when she was lowered to the ground, she couldn't make her legs hold her up and had to lean heavily against Anne, almost completely supported by her.

As soon as Mr. Nicholls dismounted, he picked Carly back up and carried her into the house.

"Walk," Carly murmured.

"I will carry you, for you are in no state to walk anywhere," said Mr. Nicholls crisply.

"Don't need a doctor to walk," Carly mumbled.

"Hush now, Caroline. We must get you out of your wet things and into bed," said Anne in a soothing tone. Mr. Nicholls put Carly on top of the covers and went back downstairs. Anne started peeling wet clothing off Carly; by the time she had wrestled free Carly's stockings and started undoing the buttons of her dress, a commotion could be heard in the hall below. Charlotte hurried into the room, the hem of her dress wet, and began to help Anne undress Carly.

"Thank goodness Mr. Nicholls found her. What was she doing so far away? It would have taken us hours to search that far on foot. Has she said anything?"

"She's very feverish," said Anne. "So nothing coherent. I hope the doctor isn't delayed."

Charlotte made no immediate reply but began rubbing Carly dry with a towel. "Fetch her nightgown, Anne, and help me get her under the covers. Tabby has some bricks heating in the oven. Is Emily back? Ask her to bring them up."

But Emily had already thought of the bricks and appeared in the doorway. She slipped the flannel-wrapped lumps into the bed and stood back to look at Carly. It wasn't an encouraging sight. Despite Anne and Charlotte's efforts to dry her, Carly's hair was still damp and lay in tangled strings across the pillow. She was pale and sweating even though her body was very cold.

"Pull the covers back, Emily, so we can get her under them," directed Charlotte.

Having secured Carly in the bed, Charlotte sat down by her side.

"You two go make some tea for the others and bring hot milk up for Caroline. If she wakes, I want to have some ready," said Charlotte. "And send Dr. Bruening up the moment he arrives."

Anne brought the milk, but Charlotte could not persuade Carly to drink—she pushed it away and moaned that her head hurt. Fortunately, the doctor soon appeared. He bustled into the room, a short rotund figure, and took Carly's wrist between his fingers.

"A bad business, Miss Brontë. Her pulse is very tumultuous. And she's obviously feverish. How long did you say she was outside?"

"About five or six hours before we were able to find her, Dr. Bruening," said Charlotte. "She'd wandered right down the valley."

"Hmm, very bad to be out in this storm," said the doctor. "It's a bad one, and no mistake. I nearly mired my gig over by the Harrisons' farm." He watched Carly for a minute, re-checked her pulse, and then clapped his hands together briskly. "I'll have to bleed her, of course. Her pulse is far too rapid and—"

But he was interrupted. Carly, feverish though she was, had heard his words.

"No!" she exclaimed. "I won't let you near if you try to bleed me!"

The doctor tried to soothe her. "My dear girl, bleeding is the only safe thing in a case like this. You are too feverish to understand what is best for you."

"No!" cried Carly again. "You can't! I don't care if it's historically accurate! It's not scientific!"

"Caroline! Please calm yourself. You are very ill and Dr. Campbell Bruening is here to help," said Charlotte, putting a soothing hand to Carly's hot forehead.

"I bet he hasn't even washed his hands! He'll give me an infection and I'll die because you people don't know about antibiotics!" sobbed Carly, who was fast becoming hysterical. "He has to wash his hands, he has to!"

The doctor turned to Charlotte and said in a low tone, "It is best to keep her as quiet as possible. She is clearly delirious." To Carly, he said in a louder tone, "Of course I will wash my hands, child. You stay here resting with Miss Brontë. I will return shortly." He stepped out of the room.

"It's science," murmured Carly, her head thrashing to and fro on the pillow.

"Hush," said Charlotte.

The doctor returned.

"No bleeding. It's not scientific," said Carly, looking at him fretfully.

"On the contrary, it is the very best science," said the doctor in a soothing tone.

"No!" cried Carly. "I don't care if you washed your hands. Bleeding won't make me better, it will make me worse!"

Dr. Bruening smoothed his waistcoat, took a step nearer and said with authority, "You know nothing of the matter. The benefits of bleeding a patient who is feverish are clearly established. You will calm yourself and trust me."

"No!" said Carly as forcefully as possible in her weakened state. She pushed herself back in the bed until she was half sitting up and held out her arm, palm towards the doctor. "You won't come near me. You won't!"

Charlotte started up in alarm. "Please lie back down, Caroline. It is not good for you to exert yourself. Hysterics will only make you worse."

"No! I won't lie down until he promises not to bleed me. He's not even my real doctor! I want Dr. Crawford!" Carly scrabbled at the covers, trying to throw them back so she could get out of bed, but she was too confused to manage it. She collapsed against the headboard, crying weakly.

Emily had entered the room during this outburst. She looked at Carly, and then the doctor. "I never saw the benefit in bleeding," she said coolly. "Surely we can wait to see if it becomes truly necessary?"

The doctor shook his head and pulled Charlotte away from the bed. Emily stepped closer, too.

"This agitation is most unhealthy. I think the best thing for now is keep her quiet. I will give you a tincture to help her sleep. The fever will get worse before we can hope to see any improvement. Give her lemonade or water and I will visit again tomorrow. Perhaps the delirium will have passed and she will hold still for a bleeding. If her pulse remains high, we may have no choice but to hold her down."

He paused. Emily and Charlotte nodded, and Charlotte gestured for him to continue.

"If her fever spikes, use wet cloths to cool her. It is too soon to tell if her lungs will become inflamed. We must hope not. Indeed, we will have to wait a day or two to see how bad this illness becomes."

Charlotte nodded. "Thank you for your help, Doctor. I think I ought to stay here, but please stop downstairs for a cup of tea with my father if you have the time."

"Not today, thank you, Miss Brontë. I must be on my way. Remember, don't be alarmed if the fever worsens tonight . . . and for the next few days."

With that, Emily escorted the doctor downstairs. Carly laid back on her pillow, still murmuring the word "science" in fretful tones. Charlotte cast a worried look at her as she straightened the covers.

"Please rest, Caroline. You must be a good patient and try to do what the doctor tells you."

"How is she?" asked Anne when Charlotte joined the rest of her family in Mr. Brontë's study.

"Feverish. She wouldn't let the doctor bleed her—she kept insisting that it wasn't scientific," said Charlotte. "Most odd. I've come down to get my mending and some more candles. I must sit up with her."

"The day is very dark thanks to this wretched storm," said Anne. "It hasn't rained this hard in months."

"The first real storm of autumn," said Emily. "If that pestilential child hadn't been caught out in it, I would have welcomed its wrath and fury."

"Was the doctor able to tell you if the fever would go to her lungs?" asked Mr. Brontë.

"It is too soon to tell," said Charlotte. "But in truth, her delirium worries me most."

"Come, I will carry the candles up for you," said Anne, rising. "And tonight we can take turns sitting with her."

"Let me fetch a glass of water—Dr. Bruening left a sleeping draught," said Charlotte. Branwell gave a swift glance at his sister when she said this, but Charlotte did not notice. Emily did, however, and she stared at Branwell until he shifted uncomfortably under her gaze.

"Just so," Emily said to him.

Upstairs, Charlotte arranged a chair near the fire while Anne lit extra candles and set them on the mantle. As Anne finished, Emily slipped quietly into the room.

"Charlotte," she murmured, careful not to wake Carly, who was tossing restlessly on the bed. "You must be careful with that sleeping draught. You would have done better not to mention it in front of Branwell."

"Surely you don't think he'd . . . " said Anne, looking shocked.

"You didn't see the expression on his face," said Emily grimly.

"I will not leave it lying around," said Charlotte, looking at the little glass vial.

Emily nodded and left the room.

Carly let out a cry, and Anne and Charlotte stood as one. Charlotte took the glass of water over to the bed, put three careful drops of the draught in it, and tucked the vial into a pocket of her dress.

"Caroline, can you drink this for me?" she said softly. "It will help you sleep."

Carly opened her eyes and looked around. The room was spinning, but she could see Charlotte bending over her and Anne standing by the fireplace, watching.

"That's right," said Charlotte, propping Carly's shoulders up so she could drink. "Just a few sips."

Carly twisted her face away from the glass and moaned. "My head hurts."

"This will help. You have a chill from being outside so long. You need to rest," said Charlotte, still holding the glass to Carly's lips. Carly tried to push it away fretfully.

"No, I don't want it!"

Charlotte took a firmer grip on her shoulders and said, "You must."

"It's science, Caroline," said Anne.

"Are you sure?" mumbled Carly.

"Yes."

Slowly Carly raised a trembling hand and helped Charlotte guide the glass to her lips. She drank the whole thing, spluttering when Charlotte poured too fast.

"Now lie back and rest. I will be here if you need anything," said Charlotte, lowering Carly back to her pillow.

Throughout the afternoon and evening, Carly's fever worsened. When the sleeping draught Dr. Bruening had left wore off, she tossed and turned. Charlotte bathed her face with cool cloths, but it was temporary relief at best. Anne came to sit with Carly after dinner so Charlotte could eat and snatch a few hours' rest. When Charlotte returned close to midnight, Anne stood up and stretched.

"I gave her another dose of the medicine—she kept talking about science," whispered Anne.

"She has been saying the oddest things all afternoon—odder than normal," said Charlotte. "I did not know she had studied Greek and Roman myths, but she keeps talking about Juno."

"Poor thing. I pray this does not settle in her lungs," said Anne, looking with compassion at the bed where Carly lay.

"As do I. Before you go, help me move this screen between her and the firelight," said Charlotte.

Charlotte spent the long hours of the night sewing in front of the fire, occasionally dozing in her chair, and checking frequently on Carly. Whenever Carly awoke enough, she would help her sip water and turn her pillows to the cooler side. All night, the fever went higher, until when Emily stole into the room around five o'clock, she found Charlotte sitting by the bed, tears seeping down her cheeks.

"Is it so very bad?" Emily asked.

"I don't know," said Charlotte. Emily stood next to Charlotte and watched Carly's face—flushed with fever, the girl was frowning in her sleep.

"I can't help but remember when . . ." Charlotte paused.

"I know," said Emily. "I was younger than you, but I remember, too. But Caroline is healthier than Maria was. And better fed. *She* had no such defenses after that horrible school."

Charlotte took Emily's hand and squeezed it.

"Go get a few hours of sleep in my room. I'll wake you if she gets much worse," said Emily, pushing Charlotte towards the door. Charlotte gave Carly a look filled with concern before she left. Emily straightened the covers and sat down to watch and wait.

By dawn, Carly's fever was so high that the sisters were not sure she would wake up. They waited anxiously for the doctor, trying to keep Carly cool and quiet. When Dr. Bruening came, he looked grave and shook his head.

"She is worse than I had hoped. I ought to have bled her yesterday. I will do so at once, and hopefully it will help."

This time Carly was too delirious to realize what was happening, and Dr. Bruening easily held her arm above a bowl and let some blood into it. Emily looked disapproving but made no move to stop him. After he had bandaged Carly's arm and felt her pulse once more, he prepared to depart.

"There is nothing else to be done. Keep applying cool cloths. Keep her quiet. Give her the tincture every six hours. I will return tomorrow before church, but I do not expect any improvement for some time," he said.

Charlotte looked at her sisters. "Dr. Bruening, it is just a chill, is it not? It hasn't gone to her lungs? It isn't infectious?"

"Well, I would say it is considerably more serious than a chill, but her exposure to the cold rain is the root of the evil. So far her lungs do not sound involved, but whether that stays the case remains to be seen. There is no risk of infection—I do not think it is typhoid or scarlet fever. Her case is serious, but not hopeless."

Charlotte relaxed, allowing her tight shoulders to slump down.

"Thank you, Dr. Bruening."

"My pleasure Miss Brontë. I understand your concern."

Throughout the day Charlotte, Anne, and Emily took turns sitting with Carly and nursing her. All three watched closely for signs of improvement and listened carefully for the dreaded rattling that would show Carly's lungs were filling with fluid. Her breathing was labored but did not worsen.

In the early evening, when Charlotte had just brought Carly's medicine, Carly woke up for the first time in a day.

Emily was in the midst of asking Anne's opinion about a plot point in her book—at what point the object of her hero's passionate love should die—when Carly opened her eyes and looked straight past all three sisters.

"You're here! I'm so glad to see you. I have so many questions," said Carly, smiling. Across the room, she saw Maria silhouetted against the window.

Charlotte moved to the bed and set the glass down so she could lift Carly's shoulders up to drink. "I have been here the whole time," she said in a soothing voice.

Carly looked at her with fever-glazed eyes. "Not you, her," she said, pointing towards the window.

All three sisters looked at where Carly pointed. There was nothing to see, yet Carly continued to talk as though there was someone there.

"You don't know how hard I'm trying, but they don't understand! They *won't*," said Carly, wondering why the room wouldn't stop spinning and why Maria's features were so blurred and watery. "I told Charlotte what you said. I told her she had to write everything in her heart, but she doesn't want to. What am I going to do if I'm stuck here forever? I want to go home!"

Carly began to cry. Charlotte, Anne, and Emily looked at one another, bewildered and concerned.

"Her delirium is worse than we thought! She speaks to people who are not there," said Charlotte.

"She's right here," said Carly, pointing at Maria.

Charlotte held up the glass again and gazed at it dubiously.

"Please drink this, Caroline. You must rest," she said. Emily moved closer to the bed and Anne followed. Carly turned and spoke beseechingly to Maria.

"Maria, they won't listen to me! What am I to *do*?!"

At the name "Maria," all three Brontë sisters gasped.

"What did she say?" asked Emily, in a whisper.

Carly looked at the three living sisters.

"You must write it the way she said! Maria says you must write what's in your hearts or we will all be trapped. Why won't you listen?" She started to cry again. "Maria, I know you said I wouldn't be free, and you wouldn't be free, and neither would they if they don't do it. If Charlotte doesn't write the right *Jane Eyre* . . . or Emily doesn't finish *Wuthering Heights*, and Anne doesn't write *Agnes Grey* . . . but what am I going to do? Tell me what I have to do to make your sisters see!"

Carly reached out a hand towards the figure of Maria at the window, but the ghost either did not hear or chose not to look at her.

Charlotte, Emily, and Anne were white with shock. Charlotte's hand trembled as she held the glass to Carly's lips, and Carly, without knowing what she did, drank. She felt her limbs grow heavier and her eyes close as she slipped back into unconsciousness.

"Who told her about Maria?" asked Charlotte in a fierce whisper. She looked between her sisters and Carly's still form.

Anne and Emily shook their heads. "I can't think that Father or Branwell would have mentioned her, either," said Emily, shivering as if in a chill draft.

"Then how does she know? How?" asked Anne in frightened tones. "What does it all mean?"

All three women looked over at the window. Nothing was visible but rain dripping down the pane. Emily picked up a candle and walked around the room, peering into shadowy corners, illuminating the hidden spaces.

"There is no one here," she whispered.

"But what did she *mean*? How could . . ." Anne hesitated. "How could she know about Maria? What does she mean, that we are all trapped?"

"It is delirious nonsense," said Charlotte, sounding very unsure. "There is no other explanation."

"But how did she know Maria's name?" Anne asked.

"She's been poking around where she wasn't supposed to, most likely, and found it out," said Emily.

As if in response, Carly opened her eyes again and whispered: "Please. Please write *Jane Eyre* the right way. I need it. And Maria says you must. Promise me, please."

Charlotte bent over her and hesitated, looking into Carly's feverish eyes.

"You remind me of her," said Charlotte. "Her last illness was so dreadful . . ."

Charlotte trailed off as Carly shook her arm weakly.

"Promise. Or I'll die here," she whispered.

"I promise," said Charlotte.

Carly released Charlotte's hand and laid back, her eyes closed. "You wouldn't say it if you didn't mean it. I know that."

"Let us pray she will be spared, even though Maria and Elizabeth were not," said Anne in a hushed tone. She watched, her eyes full of unshed tears, as Carly's chest rose and fell in shallow, rapid breaths.

"Yes, we can pray," said Charlotte, rubbing her wrist where Carly's hot hand had grasped it. "Sisters, I do not pretend to understand Caroline's words, but I think we should not mention this to Father or Branwell."

Anne and Emily nodded their agreement. Charlotte looked over at the bed, forehead creased with concern. "Poor little thing. She is very frightened. I will have to keep my promise and work on this novel."

Again Emily and Anne nodded.

"Perhaps one of you could bring it to me and I will write while she sleeps."

"Of course," said Anne.

"Do you think she really saw . . ." started Emily, and trailed off. The three sisters shivered.

"I don't know," whispered Charlotte. "We must pray she recovers quickly and stops having delirious dreams. They are not right."

"But they might be true," said Emily.

CHAPTER FIFTEEN

A week passed. Carly only woke long enough to take a little water or broth. Whenever she opened her eyes, she saw Charlotte, Anne, or Emily sitting nearby—and Maria hovering at the window. In her fever she cried out to Maria to help her, but Maria never made any reply. Nothing soothed Carly but the repeated assurances of all three Brontë sisters that they were writing, and that what they were writing reflected what was in their hearts.

Dr. Bruening visited often and looked grave.

"A week already, and her fever rages on unchecked. She is very sick indeed. I expect that in the next few days there will be a crisis and she will either turn the corner or . . ." Dr. Bruening paused and rubbed his hand against his head. "Well, you know the body cannot sustain itself in such a state. The fever must break if she is to live."

"Is there anything more we can do?" asked Charlotte, biting her lip.

"Nothing that you are not already doing," said the doctor. "You and your sisters are nursing Miss Caroline with the greatest possible care, and you have kept the room admirably free from cold drafts. Miss Emily's broth has seen more than one villager through a serious illness. So, no, there is nothing more."

Charlotte hesitated and looked down at her clasped hands. "She says things sometimes . . ."

"She is delirious," said the doctor. "She would not recognize her own parents were they to return from India tomorrow. The best thing you can do is reassure her and calm any fears she has."

Charlotte nodded, but did not look satisfied. Anne came to the door.

"Miss Anne," said the doctor, nodding a greeting.

"Dr. Bruening," she said. "Do you hold out much hope?"

Dr. Bruening shook his head slowly, "You say she was perfectly healthy before this, but if the fever does not break soon, it will be bad." He paused and looked Anne over. "You must not tire yourself. I do not want more than one patient on my hands."

Anne smiled at him. "I do not do nearly as much as Charlotte and Emily. They will not let me."

"Very wise of them," said the doctor. "Your health is too delicate to bear too much of the burden of nursing."

With that, the doctor took his leave. Anne and Charlotte stood quietly in the bedroom and looked at Carly. The fever had wasted her away; she was a thin little figure beneath the blankets. Her face was flushed and her hair was lank on the pillow.

"Poor thing," said Anne. "What did Dr. Bruening say about her visions?"

"I did not really explain them. He seemed to expect her to be delirious, but I found I could not tell him that a girl we never knew until a month ago thinks she is talking to one of our dead sisters—a sister who died twenty-one years ago, and whom we have never mentioned in front of her," said Charlotte.

"It surprises me that she is so consistent in her delusion," said Anne. "So persistent that it is Maria, and that Maria wants us to write. Where could Caroline get such ideas?"

Charlotte shivered. "It is uncanny. I know it must be the fever, but still, it frightens me. And why does Caroline think *she* is trapped unless we do what Maria, I mean, Caroline, wants?"

Anne drew nearer to Charlotte, as though taking comfort from her presence. "I don't know. We must continue to pray for her."

Carly turned her head restlessly on the pillow and opened her eyes, but showed no recognition of Charlotte or Anne. She tried to speak through her cracked lips, but it was no more than a whisper.

"I need . . ."

"What do you need, Caroline? We are here," said Charlotte. "Drink some more of this broth. We will take care of you."

Carly obeyed, sipping at the cup Charlotte held. A moment later, she tried again.

"I need to read . . ."

Charlotte shook her head. "I'm afraid you cannot read now, but Anne will read aloud to you for a time if you are a good girl and finish this cup of broth."

It was Carly's turn to shake her head weakly.

"No, I need to read *Jane Eyre*. Please. Maria said so . . ." she trailed off, and her eyes closed. Squeezing her sister's hand, Anne took Charlotte's place next to the bed and smoothed the covers over Carly's still form.

"And how is your *Jane Eyre* progressing?" she asked.

"I am writing as much as I am able, given how much nursing Caroline requires," said Charlotte, rubbing her temples. "I feel I must. I cannot fail her."

Anne nodded. "I have noticed that only our reassurance that we are writing calms her. I do not pretend to understand it, but I cannot deny that it is efficacious."

"It is not only that," said Charlotte. "It is as if all the emotion of losing Maria, of losing Elizabeth, has resurfaced. It overwhelms me, and I cannot stop the words from pouring out." She looked down at her ink-stained hands. "I cannot stop the emotions behind the words, either."

Anne nodded. "I feel a similar compulsion. And Caroline is wonderfully consistent in her belief that Maria told her these things."

Charlotte sighed. "We must hope that her mind is not permanently affected by this fever. Thankfully Dr. Bruening does not think it likely."

"Go rest," said Anne. "Emily has some lunch ready for you downstairs."

Charlotte left the room and Anne settled into the chair by the fire. For a while she sewed, but then she took up a pen and drew the side table near. Carly did not stir as Anne worked away at her book.

When Emily came in a few hours later, Carly had not yet woken.

"Charlotte told me the doctor is worried that we will lose her," said Emily.

"Yes, for she has wasted away to nothing and her fever will not break. I do not know how much longer she can fight," Anne said. "Let me get you some new water. What I was using to wet the cloth for her forehead is too warm."

"No need. I brought a fresh bowl. Go, eat something. Rest. I have solved the problem Heathcliff was giving me and will now be able to finish the chapter."

Anne left Emily scribbling away in almost the same posture she herself had occupied. The day passed; Emily wrote, pausing only to wipe Carly's brow or feed her broth. As darkness fell, Anne brought Emily a cold dinner of bread, meat, and cheese. Emily ate it in haste, eager to return to her writing. She sat with Carly until almost midnight, when Charlotte came to take the night watch.

"I think there is a little change. She is more restless, and the fever is higher. Anne twice had to get me cooler water for the basin," Emily said, stretching her arms as far above her head as her corset would allow.

Charlotte hurried over to look at Carly's flushed face. "She does look worse."

"You will have a rough night of it," said Emily. "I'll stay with you for a time—there's a bit I'm working on now that I don't want to forget."

"Thank you," said Charlotte. "It is always easier with more than one nurse, even if one of the two is busy imagining ever more dreadful depths into which her hero can sink."

Emily grinned. "He is mad, truly. But even if I am distracted, tell me when you need help, and I shall return from Thrushcross Grange."

Emily proved to be right: Within a short time, Carly grew more restless, and her fever burned hotter than the sisters had ever seen it. Emily had very little time to write; she was too busy fetching cool water for Charlotte as Charlotte bathed Carly's face, arms and legs, and torso, trying to bring the fever down.

The sisters labored through the night—Anne joined them in the small hours of the morning. Carly tossed and moaned and called out for Maria to tell Charlotte, Emily, and Anne what they must do. Nothing the sisters did could soothe her, and Carly started to cry scalding tears, repeating, "We are all lost. I tried, but we are all lost!"

Charlotte looked at Anne and Emily and saw the same look of fright that she knew was on her own face.

"There is nothing we can do but pray," she whispered. Anne and Emily nodded, and the sisters sank tremulously to their knees, clasping hands in the darkness.

As dawn approached, Charlotte took Carly's hand in hers.

"Caroline, you must get better. You must try," she said, squeezing Carly's hand lightly. There was no returning pressure. "Please," Charlotte whispered, bowing her head until it rested on the edge of the bed.

"Look!" said Anne, pointing at Carly's face. At first Charlotte thought that the worst had happened. Carly's face had gone from flushed and heated to pale and grey.

"Oh, no!" she gasped.

"No, no, look!" said Anne. "She is sweating—the fever has broken!"

Charlotte stood sharply and turned away from the bed, trying to hide the tears as they coursed down her face.

"Thank you, God, for sparing her," she whispered.

Emily drew back the curtain to let the first feeble light of dawn break into the room. The three sisters stayed nearby, keeping Carly as warm and dry as they could while she sweated out the fever that had nearly killed her. She did not wake, but when the sun finally rose, she fell into what the Brontës could see was a natural sleep, completely different from the fevered delirium of the past week.

Anne and Emily crept away to bed, while Charlotte dozed in the chair next to Carly.

By the time Carly woke, hours had passed and Anne had replaced Charlotte by her bed. Anne saw Carly open her eyes and picked up a glass. When Carly shook her head, Anne smiled reassuringly.

"It's only lemonade. You must be parched—we have hardly been able to get anything into you these last days."

Carly was too weak and thirsty to talk, so she let Anne help her sip the lemonade. Though much tarter than the juice Carly was used to, it was refreshing and helped her head clear.

"How long?" she managed to croak to Anne.

"How long have you been ill? A week," Anne said, putting the glass down and using her spare hand to turn and fluff Carly's pillows.

"A *week*?!" said Carly, her voice still hardly above a whisper. The exertion made her cough.

"Here, drink ," said Anne. "You mustn't try to do too much at first. You are out of immediate danger, but you must rest so you don't have a relapse. Dr. Bruening will visit later today to see how you do."

Carly sipped the lemonade and tried to think. She was so tired, and it was such an effort even to raise her head to drink.

"Now lie down and sleep," said Anne, tucking Carly back into bed.

Carly could feel her eyelids getting heavy. There was something important she needed to know before she slept . . . but what was it?

"Jane?" she murmured, unable to keep her eyes open another moment.

"Don't fret," said Anne. "Charlotte has been writing here in this very room as she watched over you."

"Good," muttered Carly, mostly asleep. "I need Jane."

The next time she woke, Emily was sitting by the fire. When she saw Carly stir, she brought over some broth.

"Let me help you sit up to drink this," she said, her usual acerbity notably lacking.

"Thank you," said Carly. Emily said nothing. "How is Cathy?" Carly asked.

"Dead," answered Emily with relish. "But she had to be."

"Oh," said Carly. She guessed from Emily's tone that Cathy's death was an exciting event, and wished she knew the plot of *Wuthering Heights* well enough to know whether everyone was meant to take as much ghoulish delight in her demise as Cathy's creator apparently did.

Dr. Bruening came later that morning and professed himself excessively pleased with Carly's progress.

"She must stay in bed and very quiet, of course," he told Charlotte. "It will take some weeks before she can be considered truly out of danger. Any exertion could bring about a relapse. She will be listless and tired a great deal, so your task will be easier at the beginning. Only once she starts to feel better will she give you trouble."

"So the meek way she obeys our instructions is normal?" asked Charlotte, with real concern.

"Oh, yes! She is too weak at the moment to be troublesome. In fact, it will be an excellent sign of her progress when she starts to rebel against your cosseting," said Dr. Bruening. "But don't look for that for some days yet."

"And is there any sign that the delirium has left her brain permanently affected?" asked Charlotte.

"Not at all. I find her senses no longer disordered," said Dr. Bruening with conviction. "Indeed, she is completely lucid now."

After this conversation, it was a nasty shock for Charlotte to go back into the sick room and see Caroline smiling at nothing.

"Oh, Maria," she was saying. "You don't know how happy I am that they're finally doing what you said! I didn't think they would *ever* understand!"

"Caroline! To whom are you speaking?" asked Charlotte, dismay in her voice.

Carly looked over at Charlotte and smiled sleepily. "Maria, of course. I am so tired." And with that she closed her eyes and appeared to go to sleep.

Charlotte could not decide if it would be more imprudent to wake her and demand an explanation or ignore the strange conversation and hope it would fade away as Caroline recovered. She was lost in indecision when Anne entered.

"Father needs your help in his study," Anne said. "I can sit with Caroline."

"Anne, when I came in . . ." Charlotte paused.

"Yes?"

"She thought she was talking to Maria again," said Charlotte, with a despairing hand gesture.

"Oh, dear," said Anne.

Charlotte shook her head and went to see her father. Anne sat by the fireplace and read until Carly woke twenty minutes later. She looked around the room, hoping to see Maria—and instead saw Anne putting down her book. Whether it was leftover confusion from her illness or because she was still waking, Carly said, "Dang. I fell asleep before I finished talking to Maria. Have you seen her?"

Anne came over and felt her forehead. "You don't feel as though you are feverish again."

"I'm not feverish. Haven't you seen her?" asked Carly.

Anne pulled her chair nearer the bed. "No one has—for there is nothing to see. It is a delusion from your illness."

Carly bit her lip and tried to decide if she should abandon the subject or tell Anne the truth. It would be a relief to confide in someone, and Anne seemed like the most sympathetic of the Brontës—and perhaps the most likely to believe. Carly took a deep breath and spoke before she could think better of it.

"No. This isn't a crazy hallucination from the fever. Maria—your sister Maria—has appeared and talked to me almost since I got here." Seeing Anne's worried expression, Carly hastened to add, "And I'm not crazy—although I know that's what it sounds like."

Anne shook her head as if trying to clear away cobwebs. "I admit that you do not seem mad. But how did you learn of Maria and Elizabeth?"

"Who's Elizabeth?" asked Carly, confused.

"But if you have found out about Maria, you must also have heard of Elizabeth," said Anne. "I don't think we ever talk about them apart . . ."

"Is she *another* sister?" asked Carly.

"Yes. She died at the same time as Maria," said Anne.

"Maria never mentioned her," said Carly.

Anne shook her head. "It is so peculiar to hear you talk of Maria as if she were yet among us. She died more than twenty years ago, you know. I barely remember her or Elizabeth—I was only five at the time." There was a wistful note in Anne's voice, and she looked at Carly as if hoping very much that she were telling the truth.

"Well, Maria remembers all of you," said Carly. "It's why I'm stuck here—she wants me to help you." She yawned. It was exhausting to stay awake and alert for so long. "How did she and Elizabeth die? Maria was going to tell me but we were interrupted. Was it typhoid, like Bridget Martin?"

"Only partly," said Anne in a low voice. "There was a typhoid epidemic at the school which weakened Maria, but in the end consumption killed both my sisters."

How horrible, thought Carly.

"They caught it at Cowan Bridge School," continued Anne. "I was too young to be there, but Charlotte and Emily remember."

"I'm so sorry," said Carly. "It must have been awful. Did they die at school?"

"No. Father brought them home, but it was too late." Anne passed a hand over her brow. "Maria was twelve and Elizabeth almost eleven. If they had been better looked after at school . . . If the food hadn't been so unhealthy and dirty, if the staff hadn't been so unwashed and disgusting . . . Almost ten other girls died that spring." She straightened her shoulders and looked at Carly. "The whole time the headmaster spoke as if it were a judgment from God. Even today, Charlotte and Emily can barely speak of that time."

"That is *horrible*," repeated Carly—doubly thankful now that she had been lucid enough to insist that Dr. Bruening wash his hands before he examined her.

"Yes. Perhaps you can better understand our surprise then," said Anne. "Maria died so long ago—"

"I do understand. And I can see why Maria thinks you need rescuing from your past," said Carly.

"Is that what she said?" Anne asked automatically. Then she shook her head. "Listen to me, talking as though I believed in ghosts."

"Doesn't matter if you believe or not," said Carly, drawing her blanket further up her chest. "I'm trapped until I read *Jane Eyre*." Her head still hurt, and her joints ached so. She just wanted to rest for a while. "I'll probably die of consumption or typhoid or pneumonia, like everyone else here," she added.

Anne heard the querulous note in Carly's voice and said soothingly, "You will not die. You are going to get better and better. Have another drink of lemonade and rest. I'll bathe your face with cool lavender water to take away some of the headache."

"I won't get better if I don't read *Jane Eyre*," murmured Carly, putting her head back on the pillow. "I won't." But before she could protest further, she was asleep.

Anne sat back in her chair and sighed. "If only it could be true," she whispered. "I can't help but wish that it were. To know, oh, to *know* that she was watching over us!"

She felt her eyes getting hot and wiped away a tear. "Charlotte must finish her book so this poor child can read it before she worries herself into a relapse."

ᏧᎢ CHAPTER SIXTEEN ᏧᎢ

Carly woke in the late afternoon, in time to hear a hushed conversation in the hall.

"Was Dr. Bruening absolutely certain her brain hadn't been permanently affected?" asked Anne in a worried tone.

"He assured me she was completely lucid. He said it was her lungs we need to keep a careful watch over," said Charlotte.

"Then why does she keep insisting she speaks to Maria? How does she even *know* about Maria? While you were downstairs with Father, she kept saying that she was trapped here until she did what Maria wanted."

"I too thought it part of her fever, but unless Dr. Bruening is wrong, it is something else entirely," said Charlotte. "Is she feverish again?"

"No, other than her insistence that she is trapped here until your work is complete, she is her usual self," said Anne. "In fact, that is why I came to find you: Caroline remains convinced that if she doesn't read your novel, she will die of consumption or some other dreadful disease. I don't pretend to understand the connection between the two events, but the idea has her agitated."

Carly could have called out that it was because she didn't have any of the immunities that a person who grew up in the time period would have—a thought that had been haunting her now that she'd had one bout of illness. Not to mention the unsanitary conditions prevalent in the village! But she wanted to hear the rest of what the sisters would say, so she laid still and tried not to make a sound.

"I thought that if she continued to improve, I would let her start to read some of it tomorrow or the next day—I am not finished yet, but the criticism Emily made can no longer be applied. It is as though Caroline's illness and her ravings about Maria have brought every memory of that horrible time to mind. I cannot separate those emotions from what is happening in the book," said Charlotte. "The character of Helen, in particular, reminds me of Maria."

Carly gave a twitch of joy, but tried to stay quiet so the sisters wouldn't know she was awake.

"Emily has always been the most openly passionate and filled with sensibility. She will be happy to see more of those qualities in your work," Anne said. Then she turned back to the topic that most occupied her mind. "I think, even if it is all a delusion on Caroline's part, it would be wise to humor her. She is so adamant about it. Worry of any sort cannot help her recovery."

"Yes. Perhaps reading this new book—which I must call *Jane Eyre*! She spoke so incessantly of it that I find I cannot get the title out of my head—will return her fully to health," said Charlotte in a rueful tone. "Mr. Nicholls was here today, asking after Caroline."

"After Caroline, or after you?" said Anne, a hint of teasing in her tone.

"Go rest, Anne. You look tired," said Charlotte in a very dignified way.

Carly closed her eyes and pretended to be asleep as Charlotte walked into the room. She didn't want her to know she'd been eavesdropping—again.

She waited until she heard Charlotte settle herself in the chair before stretching and opening her eyes.

"Caroline, I hope you are feeling better," said Charlotte. "I have brought you some gruel."

"Gruel? I thought that was something people only ate in books," said Carly. Not to mention, those books had never described gruel as an appetizing food.

"Wherever did you get that idea? It is most nourishing, and gentle enough for an invalid—which you are at the moment," said Charlotte, helping Carly sit upright. "Emily has a special knack for preparing it. Her gruel is known to help people regain their strength after the most dire of illnesses."

Carly inspected the contents of the bowl. Gruel looked like the food equivalent of hemming sheets, but she decided not to say so aloud. If eating it would please Charlotte and convince her that Carly was well enough to start reading *Jane Eyre*, Carly would have ten bowls. She picked up the spoon, took a bite, and tried to look pleased.

Charlotte sat back with a smile. "I don't want you to tire yourself. If the bowl gets too heavy, I am happy to help. A fever like yours weakens a person terribly."

Carly was about to protest, but feeling the weight of the bowl in her hand and how it made her wrist ache, she decided that maybe Charlotte had a point. She ate half the gruel before she needed help. She was surprised how tired she was after finishing—even a small bowl of food left her ready to rest.

"Caroline," Charlotte said tentatively, helping Carly into a more comfortable position. "You must know that it is not possible for you to see and talk to our sister, Maria. If you persist in your belief, I will be forced to bring the matter up with Dr. Bruening. He says you are lucid and healing well, but he does not know you talk to spirits."

"Of course he doesn't," said Carly. "Maria has nothing to do with him, or my fever. She just wants you and your sisters to be all right. To be happy."

Charlotte looked around the room. "Do you see her right now? Can you call her to you?"

"Of course not. I'm not a witch," said Carly. "She shows up when she has something to tell me—usually something I don't want to hear—and then she disappears again. I think it's the air here. I haven't seen ghosts anywhere else. I didn't believe in them!"

"Caroline, I was with you throughout your terrible illness. There was no one in the room for that time but for me, Anne, Emily, and sometimes Dr. Bruening," said Charlotte. "We looked."

"Okay," agreed Carly. "I can't remember very much of last week, but it would be weird for Maria to show herself around other people."

"What exactly does she want from you? Or, what do you think she wants?" amended Charlotte.

"She wants you to be happy, and she knows I come from a ti—" Carly caught herself before she said "time." Charlotte was worried enough about the ghost; no need to bring up time travel, too. "A place where it is allowable to be angry and sad about bad things that happened to you, a place where we know talking about those emotions helps get rid of them."

Carly couldn't help a yawn—the concentration needed to explain things to Charlotte was making her head hurt. Charlotte arranged the pillows more comfortably, and sat looking at Carly for a long moment.

"I cannot bring myself to believe that you have spoken to Maria," she said. "But I also cannot deny that writing my novel in a way that utilizes the emotions your talk of her has recalled to me is a relief."

"Then maybe I won't die here," said Carly, half asleep already.

"I very much hope you will not," said Charlotte. "Rest now. When you are stronger, I will let you read some of the book and tell me if you think Maria would approve."

"No problem," said Carly, snuggling under the blankets and closing her eyes. She heard Charlotte move her chair away from the bedside toward the fireplace. *I hope she's going to do some writing and not hem any sheets*, thought Carly, but her eyes were too comfortably closed to open them and check. *Gruel and sheets* was the last thing that flitted through her mind before she fell asleep.

The fever had so weakened Carly that she slept a good deal and could not get out of bed without assistance. She did not need constant attendance, however, so the routine of the parsonage went back to normal—though Charlotte spent a great deal of time with Carly, whose appetite remained poor. Emily's gruel did seem to be doing some good, though. Carly was slowly able to eat more of it, as well as chicken broth and plain toast.

After two days like this, Carly felt well enough to sit up in bed. She waited until Charlotte and Anne had finished fussing over her and Anne had left. Then she looked at Charlotte and said, "Can I please read your book now? It would help me feel better."

Charlotte looked searchingly at her. "Why do you want to read *my* book so much? Why not the novels that Emily or Anne are writing?"

"I told you—Maria said I'm stuck here until I read *Jane Eyre*. Your sisters have to write those books for me to get home, but I don't have to read them. Yet. I'm sure I'll read them once they're published," said Carly.

"But you will remain here until your parents return from India, whether or not I let you read my work," said Charlotte.

Carly shook her head. "You'll just think I'm feverish again if I try to explain. Can't you let me read it? If I'm right, it will all sort itself out, and if I'm still suffering from delusions, then at least you'll be humoring a sick girl."

Charlotte couldn't help but smile as she leaned back in her chair. "Well, because I don't want you to have a relapse, I will let you read the first chapters today."

"Thank you!" said Carly, exuberant.

She had done it! She was going to read *Jane Eyre* and get home! Maybe even today! Carly wasn't sure if she just had to re-read the part of the book she'd read in the bookstore or if she had to read more—maybe even the whole thing. It didn't matter; knowing the pages would soon be in her hands was a good feeling.

Charlotte returned with the chapters, but before she handed them over, she looked sternly at Carly. "You will only be allowed to read this if you do not let yourself get too excited. If you seem at all worse after reading, I won't let you have any more. You are still weak and must be careful."

"I will be, I promise! If I get too tired, I'll stop and rest," said Carly, trying to look very trustworthy and responsible.

"Hmm," was all Charlotte said in reply, but she handed the pages over nonetheless. While Carly read, she sat by the fireplace and wrote.

Carly found it as hard to read as the other things she'd looked at from this time period; it too was handwritten, with various things crossed out and added to the margins, and Charlotte's handwriting was vastly different from anything Carly was used to seeing at home. It forced her to read slowly, rather than rushing through the way she wanted. And instead of skipping around the way she had in the bookstore, Carly read the pages straight through.

She felt a thrill when she got to the part she recognized.

"I soon possessed myself of a volume, taking care that it should be one stored with pictures . . ."

I'm reading the first draft of Jane Eyre, she thought. *This is so cool. Francesca won't believe it when I tell her!*

It felt like no time at all had passed before she had finished. She looked at Charlotte, who was now busy sewing.

"May I read some more?" she asked.

"Not today. You must rest."

Carly wanted to read as much as Charlotte had written as fast as she could, but she had to admit that her eyes were sore from the strain of deciphering the script and she was starting to feel dizzy.

"I'm thirsty," she murmured.

"Here is some water, and Emily is making more gruel for your lunch."

Carly drank the water and tried to think nice things about gruel. It was an uphill battle. After she ate, she was tired enough to be glad to nap. Just the effort of sitting up to read, then sitting up again for lunch, exhausted her. She dozed through the afternoon, only waking up for lemonade and toast at tea time.

Her recovery was slow, but steady. She usually felt better in the morning and was tired by the afternoon. She couldn't sleep through the night—she needed to have her pillows plumped and drink water or warm milk to go back to sleep—but she no longer required constant attendance, and so Charlotte was finally able to catch up on her sleep.

As Carly got better, she slept less during the day and found being confined to bed more and more irksome. It was only her steady progress through *Jane Eyre* that kept her from going stir-crazy. Each day, Charlotte would give her two or three new chapters to read, and the book was so exciting that Carly always begged Charlotte for more.

Soon, Carly found herself wondering how many chapters there would be. It had been almost a week, and Carly could tell there was lots of story left. Carly kept expecting to see Maria, but she never appeared.

Whenever I see her, it means something has gone horribly wrong with the plan, so it's probably a good sign . . . or maybe it's just that I can't get a minute alone these days, she thought.

Dr. Bruening visited periodically. Carly always asked him if he'd washed his hands and when she would be allowed to go downstairs—or even outside. Watching the dreary autumn weather out the window hadn't made her *particularly* eager to be outdoors, but she didn't want Dr. Bruening to keep her cooped up in her room longer than necessary.

"Well, Caroline, I am very pleased with your progress," the good doctor finally said. "I think you may go downstairs tomorrow."

"Really?" asked Carly, excited to see something besides the view from her bedroom window.

"Yes, yes, as long as you are kept warm and away from drafts, I see no harm in it. You gave us all quite a fright, but you are improving rapidly."

"This is rapid?" asked Carly. Her convalescence had dragged on intolerably, she thought.

"Very. And now that you are doing better, you may stop taking the paregoric draught you dislike so much," said Dr. Bruening.

"Oh, thank you! That stuff is so disgusting!" said Carly. She looked at the little glass bottle on the mantelpiece with barely concealed hatred.

"I did not prescribe it because it is delicious—I prescribed it because it helped you return to health faster," said Dr. Bruening. Carly shrugged her shoulders—of course he didn't care if it tasted vile, he wasn't the one who had to take it.

After much pestering by Carly, the sisters finally agreed to let her come downstairs for a limited time . . . but only after Dr. Bruening assured them it was safe so long as she was kept warm. Thus Carly's first trip downstairs after her illness was attended by endless preparations—so endless that Carly eventually asked Charlotte, "Will I make it downstairs before dinner, do you think?"

And in fact it was almost dinnertime when she was allowed to come slowly and carefully down the stairs. The fuss was enough to make her glad to sit down in the armchair near the fire in Mr. Brontë's study. Anne wrapped a shawl around her shoulders and Charlotte brought her dinner on a tray.

"Shall I stay with you while you eat, Caroline?" Charlotte asked.

"Oh, no, please go eat with everyone else in the dining room," said Carly. "I'm warm as can be, and I'll call if I need anything."

So Charlotte left her to eat her dinner slowly in front of the fire. Carly wasn't looking forward to climbing back up the stairs, and so ate all of her food even though she wasn't very hungry. She was determined to give herself the strength to get back up to bed without having to be carried.

That night before she fell asleep, she asked Charlotte how much of *Jane Eyre* was left to read.

"I intend to write the Epilogue tonight, so it is thirty-eight chapters, all told," Charlotte answered.

"Does that mean I can read the ending tomorrow?" asked Carly, sitting up in bed.

"Yes, but only if you lie back down and go to sleep immediately," said Charlotte.

Carly promptly lay back down, but couldn't help giving an excited wiggle under the bedclothes. Tomorrow! Tomorrow was the day she'd get home! She had used some of the time she'd been forced to lie in bed to count up the days she'd been away from her family, and was shocked to realize it had been more than a month.

A month! thought Carly. *I hope time hasn't been moving as fast back home, or Francesca and my parents will think I'm dead.*

Carly fell asleep still worrying over the complexities of time travel, but her outing downstairs had tired her enough that she slept through the night. In the morning, she woke up feeling more like her old self than she had since her ill-fated ramble on the moors. She smiled brightly at Anne when she brought in breakfast, and asked when she could go downstairs again.

Anne smiled back. "Your excursion yesterday does not seem to have harmed you, so I imagine Charlotte will let you come down again for the afternoon," she said. "My father's study is the best room to keep you warm and out of drafts in this chilly autumn weather, but he is using it this morning. This afternoon, however, Branwell will accompany him to the village, and the study will be at your disposal."

Not until the afternoon! Being forced to wait disappointed Carly, but she was happy to avoid seeing Branwell. She hadn't forgotten his horrible words the day she'd gotten lost on the moors—or his cruel mockery of her French and German abilities.

With Anne's assistance, Carly dressed and went to her chair by the window. *Oh, well,* she thought. *Maybe Charlotte will bring me the last chapters to read up here. I suppose it doesn't matter where I finish it.*

But Carly felt like it *did* matter—it made sense to come full circle and finish reading *Jane Eyre* in the chair in which she had first appeared at the parsonage.

She spent the morning in nervous anticipation. Finally, Emily brought up a light lunch; after Anne, who ate at a normal pace, finished, Charlotte came up to say that Mr. Brontë and Branwell had left, and to help Carly down the stairs.

While she was walking slowly and carefully down, Carly realized that if this worked, if reading the end of *Jane Eyre* brought her home, she would never see any of the Brontës again.

"Oh!" she said aloud.

"Are you well?" asked Charlotte, pausing.

"Yes," said Carly looking at Charlotte next to her, and Anne and Emily just behind—Anne carrying a shawl for Carly's shoulders and a blanket for her lap, while Emily held the lunch dishes on a tray. "Yes, I'm fine. I just . . ." she paused. What could she say that wouldn't make the sisters think she was getting feverish again? If she said a proper goodbye, they would probably send her straight back to bed.

"I just wanted to thank you—all three of you—for everything you've done for me," she said haltingly.

Emily looked surprised, and Anne and Charlotte looked touched. "You are very welcome, Caroline. We are all happy to see you regaining your health so quickly," said Charlotte, patting Carly's hand. Carly smiled back and continued her careful progress down the stairs.

Charlotte helped Carly get comfortably settled in an arm-chair by the fire. Looking out the window, Carly thought the weather looked just like Juneau's on the day she'd come to Haworth—cold, grey, and rainy. After Charlotte had made sure there was no possibility Carly could catch cold, Carly looked pleadingly at her.

"Did you finish? May I read it please?"

"I did finish it—I've never written anything so quickly," said Charlotte.

"Perhaps it was not having to spend most of your day trying to help me understand horrible German grammatical rules," suggested Carly.

"Perhaps," Charlotte said with a smile. "I'll go and fetch it for you."

When she returned with the last chapters, Carly took them in trembling hands.

"Thank you," she almost whispered. "Thank you for doing this for me. I can't believe . . ."

"I must go help Emily in the kitchen, but call if you need anything," said Charlotte. "I hope you enjoy the ending."

For a short time after Charlotte left, Carly sat with the pages on her lap and stared into the fire. Then she gave her head a shake and started to read. She was dying to get home, but *Jane Eyre* was so good that she didn't want it to be over; she read the last few chapters with a mixture of delight and reluctance.

The novel ended exactly the way she'd hoped, and as she reached the last few pages, she felt her eyes grow heavy. This time she did not try to fight it, but let them drift closed. The last words she read were,

"On that occasion, he again, with a full heart, acknowl-edged that God had tempered judgment with mercy."

For a long time there was no noise but Carly's steady breathing. Then, slowly, a voice spoke to her in her sleep. Maria's voice.

"Thank you Carly—you have freed us, and so you have freed yourself. Thank you."

"Mmm," muttered Carly.

A new voice intruded.

"I've never known anyone to fall asleep reading *Jane Eyre* before! I consider it a very exciting book."

Carly shook her head to clear away the cobwebs. "I'm not asleep," she said.

"Then why are your eyes closed?" said the voice. "If you're going to be dozing by my fire, you hand that precious book right back before you drop it!"

Carly sat up, fully awake. Could it be? Yes, there was the old bookseller! Carly stood, hardly able to believe it.

"I'm back!" she said.

"What do you mean? You were never gone. I left the room for two minutes to see to a customer, and when I came back you were asleep with my precious first edition about to slide out of your hands and go thump on the floor!" said the old man, taking the book back tenderly.

"That's exactly what people left behind always say!" Carly crowed.

She looked down to see what she was wearing—the same clothes she'd had on when she and Nan and her family got back from their camping trip. Her rubber boots were even still damp.

"Where's—" Carly started to say, but at that moment Francesca appeared from around a bookshelf.

"Francesca!" Carly practically threw herself on her best friend and gave her a giant hug. "Nan!" She cried again. In her excitement, she grabbed Francesca and started shaking her by the shoulders.

"What? What's going on?" asked Francesca, her teeth rattling from Carly's enthusiastic greeting.

"You girls can catch up outside. I'm closing for the day," said the old man.

Before they knew it, the old man had bustled them out amongst the shelves, picked up Carly's wet bag off the floor by the door, and waved a cheerful goodbye as he bundled them out onto the stoop.

"Wait! Wasn't it you who sent me—"

But the old man shut the door in Carly's face before she could finish her question.

"Francesca, come on! I have the most tickety-boo thing *ever* to tell you!" Carly clasped her best friend's hand in delight, and then dragged her down the street toward a nearby coffee shop. "You're going to die when you hear."

"What is it? I was only gone about five minutes," said Francesca, hurrying to keep up.

"I know! That's how it always works."

"How *what* always works? You're not making any sense," Francesca said.

"Francesca. I did it. I went into a book!" Carly stopped in the middle of the sidewalk on Main Street. Francesca stopped with her, narrowing her eyes.

"For real? Into a book? And it's no fair teasing."

"Well, not the book itself," amended Carly. "But I started reading *Jane Eyre* and then I wound up in 1846 and Charlotte Brontë was my governess!"

"No way!" exclaimed Francesca. "Why didn't I get to go too?"

"I don't know, and I missed you *so much*." Carly was hopping up and down in excitement.

"Do you *swear* this is real and not one of your pretends?"

Carly calmed herself down enough to answer seriously. "I swear, Nan."

Francesca knew her friend well enough to see that she meant every word.

"Okay, tell me everything! What was it like? What were you wearing? What did you do? I haven't read *Jane Eyre*; is it good? How long were you there? Were there m⬛⬛⬛⬛s?" Francesca had a million questions and she couldn't get them out fast enough.

"I'll tell you all about it—let's get a hot cocoa and go back to my house. I have to get that camp application ready. I promised I'd apply if I got home," said Carly, beginning to walk again.

"You're going to apply? Yay!" said Francesca, momentarily diverted. "I bet your essay will be the best—who else can say they decided to apply while vacationing in 1846? Did you have to ride a horse back then?"

"And learn French and German. Ugh."

"I am *so* jealous," sighed Francesca.

"We've got to find that bookshop again. Then we can read a book together. Maybe The *Lion, the Witch, and the Wardrobe* . . . No, wait, *The Ordinary Princess* . . . No . . . Man, I want to read all the books!"

"Yeah, all the books!" agreed Francesca.

The two friends hurried up the street, talking as fast as they could.

So quietly they didn't hear it over their chatter, a voice whispered, "All the books? Such ambition. We'll see . . ."

Acknowledgments

I could not have written *Braving the Brontës* without the help and encouragement of many people. Most importantly, thank you, Carey and Saira, and everyone at In This Together Media, for working so hard on the first book in the **Carly Keene: Literary Detective** series; it has been an honor. Genevieve Gagné-Hawes provided invaluable assistance throughout the writing and editing of this book. My parents read early drafts and had many astute comments. My husband, Bryan, laughed in all the right places, and made sure our children didn't become feral while I was finishing. Thanks to Brett Kopelan for being a benefactor.

Author's Note

While I have tried to draw a faithful portrait of the Brontës and their time, there are several places where I have taken liberties with the timing of events, or added details for reasons of continuity and plot. For example, Anne and Emily had already sent out *Agnes Grey* and *Wuthering Heights* to publishers by August 1846 (they were rejected), and there is no record of M. Heger ever responding to Charlotte's letters as I had him do here.

There are several excellent biographies of the Brontës. The most comprehensive and the one on which I relied most heavily in my research is Juliet Barker's recently revised *The Brontës, Wild Genius on the Moors: The Story of a Literary Family* (Pegasus Books, 2010). If you prefer something shorter, Catherine Reef wrote a Young Adult biography titled *The Brontë Sisters: The Brief Lives of Charlotte, Emily, and Anne* (Clarion Books, 2012). Below is a brief sketch of the Brontë family's history, followed by Book Club Questions.

A Brief History of the Brontës

Charlotte, Anne, and Emily Brontë were responsible for some of the 19th century's most treasured literature, including

Charlotte's *Jane Eyre*, Emily's *Wuthering Heights*, and Anne's *Agnes Grey*. Patrick and Maria Brontë had 6 children, beginning with Maria in 1814, and followed by Elizabeth, Charlotte, Patrick Branwell, Emily, and Anne. Patrick's wife Maria died in 1821, shortly after the birth of Anne. Maria and Elizabeth, the two eldest daughters, both died of tuberculosis at a very young age.

The remaining three sisters worked on and off throughout their life as both teachers and governesses. In February of 1842, Charlotte and Emily Brontë went to Brussels to study at a boarding school run by Monsieur and Madame Heger. Although they had to return home due to the death of their aunt, Charlotte went back to the school to continue her studies. She returned home by 1845, reuniting with her siblings, though she was thought to be in love with the schoolmaster, Monsieur Heger, and continued to write him letters. By this time, Branwell was addicted to alcohol and opium (laudanum).

The sisters published a book of poems in 1846, entitled *Poems* by Currer, Ellis, and Acton Bell. Despite the use of their pen names (which were purposefully masculine in order to increase their chances of being published), the book only sold two copies. However, Charlotte went on to write *Jane Eyre*, published in 1847, Emily wrote *Wuthering Heights*, published in 1847, and Anne wrote *Agnes Grey*, published in 1847 and *The Tenant of Wildfell Hall*, published in 1848. Branwell and Emily both died of tuberculosis in 1848, while Anne died of the same disease in 1849.

Charlotte, the only Brontë child left, continued to live with her father and write. She went on to write *Shirley*, published in 1849, and *Villette*, published in 1853. The following year she married her father's curate, Arthur Bell Nicholls, but died shortly after in 1855 of the same disease that took the lives of all of her siblings.

Books and authors mentioned in *Braving the Brontës*:

The Nancy Drew series by Carolyn Keene
The Adventures of Sherlock Holmes by Sir Arthur Conan Doyle
The Chronicles of Narnia by C.S. Lewis
Rilla of Ingleside by L. M. Montogmery
The Railway Children, Five Children and It, The Enchanted Castle by E. Nesbit
The Harry Potter series by J. K. Rowling
The Ordinary Princess by M. M. Kaye
Jane Eyre by Charlotte Brontë
Little Women by Louisa May Alcott
The Secret Garden by Frances Hodgson Burnett
Poems by Currer, Ellis, and Acton Bell
Pride and Prejudice by Jane Austen
A Little Princess by Frances Hodgson Burnett
Caddie Woodlawn by Carol Ryrie Brink
The *Little House* series by Laura Ingalls Wilder
Anne of Green Gables by L. M. Montgomery
The Phantom of the Opera by Gaston Leroux
Rob Roy by Sir Walter Scott
Wuthering Heights by Emily Brontë
The Pilgrim's Progress by Paul Bunyan
Swallows and Amazons by Arthur Ransome
Agnes Grey by Anne Brontë
Alphabet Flore by Pierre-Joseph Redouté

Book Club Questions

How do you think Francesca and Carly's feeling of being watched at the beginning of the novel plays into Carly's adventure with the Brontës?

Both Francesca and Carly long for a life more like that of a romantic heroine from a novel. Why do you think they desire this? In your opinion, what qualities make up the ideal heroine?

Why do you think the Brontë sisters were so defensive about their brother, Branwell, who clearly had issues with drugs and alcohol?

Why do you think the reputation of Branwell would affect the sisters' ability to open a school?

Maria continually tells Carly she must help "free the Brontës from the past." In your opinion, what does being "freed from the past" mean?

Carly is constantly getting reprimanded in the Brontë's house for speaking out of place. Do you think her decision to continue to speak out was necessary? Could she have spoken in a way that wouldn't have offended the Brontës?

Do you think Carly's adventure with the Brontës was "real" or a dream?

What are some challenges, besides the ones mentioned in the story, you might face if you went back in time to 1846?

If you could go back in time, what year would you travel to and why?

About Katherine Rue

Born and raised in Alaska, Katherine will happily tell you what to do in a variety of survival situations, including but not limited to: bear attacks, hypothermia, nettle stings, and how to start a fire in the rain. She received a B.A. in Classics from Dartmouth College and a Masters in Medieval History from The University of California, Berkeley. She lives against her better judgment in New York City (which she cordially dislikes) with her husband and sons (whom she likes, very much). This is her first book.

Other Books by
In This Together Media

The Soccer Sisters Series by Andrea Montalbano
　　Lily Out of Bounds
　　Vee Caught Offside
　　Tabitha One on One

Kat McGee Adventure Series
　　Kat McGee and The School of Christmas Spirit
　　by Rebecca Munsterer
　　Kat McGee and The Halloween Costume Caper
　　by Kristin Riddick
　　Kat McGee Saves America
　　by Kristin Riddick

Playing Nice by Rebekah Crane
Aspen by Rebekah Crane

Personal Statement by Jason Odell Williams

Be A
Noble
kid

Reading Guide
By Kati Robins

CHAPTER 1

Vocabulary Words: tone, sedate, cursory, devolved, bout, skiff, mature, remorse, sidling, tribulation, ferry

Discussion Questions:

1. What is Carly and Francesca's favorite phrase?

_____

What is the origin of the phrase, and what does it mean?

_____

_____

2. When Carly and Francesca leave the tent to investigate, they pretend that they are Nancy Drew and Sherlock Holmes.

Who is Nancy Drew?

_____

_____

Who is Sherlock Holmes? _____

_____

3. "Adventures in real life were harder to come by than books always made it seem." What does this phrase mean, **and** do you agree, or disagree?

_____

_____

_____

4. Francesca's mom has a lot of "Nutritional Rules." Do you have any "Nutritional Rules" in your household? If so, what are they?

_____

_____

What are some benefits of having "Nutritional Rules"?

_____

_____

_____

5. Carly and Francesca consider that the mysterious voice and movement may be an enchanted wizard otter or alien. What, or who, do you think it is?

Activities:

Create a character journal that includes three columns: Character Name, Facts and Characteristics, and Portrait. Each time you meet a new character, add their name to the journal. As you read and get to know each of them, list details about their lives, their families, their physical characteristics, and their personality traits. Then draw a portrait of each character.

Carly would have preferred an older brother like Rilla had in *Rilla of Ingleside* by L. M. Montgomery. Add the *Anne of Green Gables* series by L. M. Montgomery to your reading list and discover who Rilla's brother is and why Carly would want him as an older brother.

Draw a picture of a skiff, and identify the gunwale, stern, and bow.

Science Connection: Carly's campsite was near a dense forest comprised of spruce, alder, and hemlock trees that formed a barrier to the interior of the island. Research one of these tree types. Include a photo, its Genus and Family name, its physical characteristics, its uses, and regions where it can be found.

CHAPTER 2

Vocabulary Words: idly, immersion, confident, stubborn, exasperation, beckoning, protocol, patron, bemoaned, indignantly, stupefied, pinafore

Discussion Questions:

1. Why is Carly so hesitant to go to the French Immersion Camp?

_____

_____

Have you ever been hesitant to participate in something because of your insecurities? Explain.

_____

_____

_____

2. What did the girls discover on their walk back to Carly's house?

_____

3. Carly and Francesca knew that they had to explore the mysterious alleyway because they had read "all of the right books." What does this mean?

_____

_____

_____

Have you ever read a book by C. S. Lewis, E. Nesbit, or J. K. Rowling? If so, which one(s)?

_____

4. What is the name of the book that is presented to Carly by the old man in the mysterious bookstore?

_____

What is so special about the copy that the man presents to Carly?

_____

5. What is a pen name?

_____

What pen names did Charlotte, Emily, and Anne Brontë use?

_____

_____

6. When Carly awakens from her slumber, everything has changed. Where do you think she is, <u>and</u> what do you think will happen next?

_____

_____

_____

Activities:

Visit your local bookstore or library to see if they have an original copy of *The Ordinary Princess* by M. M. Kaye. Look inside to see if it has color illustrations.

If you had authored a book, wouldn't you want the whole world to know that you had written it? Do some investigating, and see if you can find the reason(s) why all of these women would have used pen names instead of their own. In paragraph form in the space below, share your findings.

_____

_____

_____

_____

_____

_____

CHAPTER 3

Vocabulary List: punctuality, virtue, slouched, incautious, dolt, bitter, clamoring, competent, peril, reformed, mirthless, wuthering, resolutely

Discussion Questions:

1. Where is Carly? _____

2. What is the moor? _____

3. Carly has finally found herself immersed in a mysterious adventure, with a name suitable for a heroine, and yet it's not at all what she expected and she is having a difficult time enjoying it. Have you

ever found yourself possessing something or in a situation that you always wanted, but found it to be less desirable than you thought it would be? Explain.

_____

_____

_____

_____

Activities:

Create a list of all the clues in this chapter that inform you that Carly has found herself in a very different time period.

<u>CHAPTER 4</u>

Vocabulary List: surreptitiously, defiantly, dubious, yoke, glowering, resolved, imposter, tedious, dismayed, render, melancholy, appalling, taper, indisposition, chided

Discussion Questions:

1. What year is it in the book?

_____

2. Why do you think Carly's favorite part of Queen Elizabeth the First's speech at Tilbury is when she says she "has the heart and stomach of a king"?

_____

_____

3. When Charlotte told Carly that her French pronunciation was dreadful, Carly felt a "surge of shame that she couldn't do it as easily as she did the rest of her schoolwork". Can you relate to how Carly must have felt? Explain.

_____

_____

_____

_____

Activities:

While Carly ate breakfast in silence, she studied the various Brontës who were seated at the table. Create a drawing of the breakfast table using the description in this chapter, and place each person in attendance in their correct position.

Look up Queen Elizabeth the First's speech to the troops at Tilbury when she thought the Spanish Armada was coming, copy or print it, and recite it in front of an audience.

Copy the poem **Lines Composed in a Wood on a Windy Day** by Anne Brontë on the left side of a large piece of white construction paper. On the right side of the paper, create an illustration that depicts the meaning of the poem.

In a group, discuss and decipher the meaning of the poem *Stanzas* by Emily Brontë.

CHAPTER 5

Vocabulary List: parsonage, acerbic, oblige, diligent, meander, exuberance, foliage, abominably, querulous, proficient, deficiency, impenetrable, thicket, drudgery, penury, balderdash, chastened

Discussion Questions:

1. How do you think Charlotte feels about Jane Austen, and why do you think she feels that way?

_____

_____

2. Carly wondered if Charlotte and her sisters felt trapped by their duties. What do you think? Explain.

_____

_____

_____

3. In the books that Carly's grandmother gave to her, the heroines were always prim and proper, and very charming. However, in the books that Carly's mother gave her, the heroines were not proper at all. Why do you think there was such a difference in the depiction of the heroines?

_____

_____

_____

4. What is laudanum, <u>and</u> from what does Branwell suffer?

_____

_____

5. What did Carly discover as she eavesdropped on the sisters?

_____

_____

6. Carly finally met the voice and presence she had been feeling. Who was it, <u>and</u> what did she say?

_____

_____

_____

Activities:

Carly watched the movie *Pride and Prejudice* whenever her grandmother would visit. Rent and watch the movie *Pride and Prejudice*, then write a one-page review of the film.

OR

Read the book, *Pride and Prejudice* by Jane Austen, and then watch the movie. Compare and contrast the storylines, and explain which one you enjoyed more, and why. Extension: How did the effect of reading this story in a book compare or contrast to the effect of how the film conveyed the story using techniques such as lighting, sound, color, or specific camera work.

Carly is very much enjoying reading the poems that the Brontë sisters have written. Read some of their poems yourself and decide which sister's poetry you prefer.

Social Studies Connection: On a map, measure the distance between Juneau, Alaska and Yorkshire, England.

Math Connection: How many years are between 2013 and 1846?

Carly believes that she has seen a ghost. Formulate an argument that either supports the existence of ghosts, or one that maintains that ghosts are solely fictional characters. Present your argument to the class.

*Don't forget to keep track of the different characters in your character journal!

CHAPTER 6

Vocabulary List: hefted, vulgarity, refrain, infirm, privy, heathen, gallivanting, subdued, impertinent, unobtrusive, imprudence, vexing, indignation, thwarted, absconded, berth

Discussion Questions:

1. The conditions that Carly encounters while visiting the ill or the poor are less than desirable: the sewer out in the open, and the "grave water." After reading about the conditions in 1846, what modern conveniences are you grateful to have?

_____

_____

_____

_____

2. When Charlotte overheard the comments made about her brother by the two women passing by, how do you think it made her feel?

_____

_____

3. Carly is shocked by the death of Bridget Martin, but the others do not seem to be. In 1846, why do you think the death of children and adults would be a common occurrence?

_____

_____

4. "When grown-ups didn't want to let kids see what was wrong, Carly thought, it usually meant the trouble lay with their hearts." What does this sentence mean?

_____

_____

5. Carly believes that the Brontës are acting very childish, and wants to confront them about it. Have you ever witnessed adults acting childish? If so, did you confront them about their behavior? Why, or why not?

_____

_____

_____

6. Charlotte receives a letter and becomes distraught. Who do you think the letter is from <u>and</u> what do you think it says?

_____

_____

7. Why is this time period called the Victorian Era?

_____

_____

8. Carly is so upset by everyone's behavior, and is growing increasingly homesick. If you could talk to Carly, what advice would you give her?

_____

_____

_____

Activities:

Consider how Carly must be feeling after everything that has happened. Write a journal entry as if you were Carly, from her point of view, expressing your thoughts and feelings about the events that have occurred.

Carly and Charlotte visit many people who are sick or poor, and deliver baskets full of food or items that will help them. Lead a philanthropic effort among your peers: organize a canned food drive and collect non-perishable foods to donate to a local food bank, make rainbow loom bracelets or get well cards to donate to a local children's hospital, or collect old blankets and towels to donate to a local animal shelter. Follow Carly and Charlotte's example and give to those in need!

Science Connection: Charlotte told Carly not to touch her dress after visiting the Martins because "Bridget Martin has typhoid", a disease that we don't face today. Do some research and find out what typhoid is, and what other diseases and illnesses were common in 1846. Do those illnesses still exist today? Why, or why not?

CHAPTER 7

Vocabulary List: ominous, brandished, prattle, dote, feigning, haggard, scrutiny, reconciled, obliged

Discussion Questions:

1. When the ghost appears again, she says, "There is no hope if you do not free them." Who do you think Carly is supposed to free, or save?

2. What makes Carly thankful for her brother, James?

_____

_____

3. What did Carly do that made her feel guilty?

_____

_____

Do you think what she did was right or wrong? Explain.

_____

_____

4. Have you read *The Pilgrim's Progress* by John Bunyan, or *Little Women* by Louisa May Alcott? If so, what did you think? If not, put them on your reading list.

_____

_____

_____

5. When Charlotte says, "It is the way of the world. While that ought not to affect us, I am afraid our courage was not equal to risking society's scorn for disappointed hopes." what does she mean?

_____

_____

Activities:

In this chapter, Carly tries desperately to time travel back home. Make a list of other literary characters that have traveled in time.

CHAPTER 8

Vocabulary List: equanimity, quelled, specter, catharsis, consternation, impudent, askance, decorous, benevolence, demur

Discussion Questions:

1. Carly's favorite book is *Swallows and Amazons* by Arthur Ransome. What is your favorite book?

_____

2. What are the three problems that Carly has?

    1. _____

    2. _____

    3. _____

3. Who is the ghost, and what does she tell Carly to do?

_____

_____

4. What character trait does Mr. Nicholls possess that Carly describes as "indispensible in a husband"?

_____

5. What do you predict will happen next?

_____

_____

_____

Activities:

Carly makes many references to books that she has read, and characters in those books. Create a list comprised of the references she makes, and sort them into two columns: Already Read, and Haven't Read Yet. Spend your summer vacation experiencing some of the journeys and adventures that Carly has by reading some of the same books.

CHAPTER 9

Vocabulary List: enquire, amiss, censure, savage, transgressions, admonished, solicitor

Discussion Questions:

1. Why were the Brontës so "horrified" by Carly's line of questioning at the dinner table?

_____

_____

How did their reactions make Carly feel?

_____

2. What is Carly's motivation for wanting to learn how to knit?

_____

3. Carly has formulated a plan that will help her complete the tasks that Maria has charged her with. What is her plan, <u>and</u> do you think it will work? Why, or why not?

_____

_____

_____

_____

Activities:

Complete a Venn diagram listing the similarities and differences of life in 1846 and the present, using examples from Carly's experiences with the Brontës.

Life in 1846 is very different from life today. Research something that you find to be particularly strange, or interesting, about life back then? Share your findings with your class.

<u>CHAPTER 10 and CHAPTER 11</u>

Vocabulary List: contrition, decorum, deplored, persevered, premonition, outlandish, hypocrisy, bewilderment, bland, inept, grisly, endowed, repentant, tartly, pious, intrigue, compelling

Discussion Questions:

1. When Carly visits the bookstore, she is surprised to find that the shop only has a few novels and stories. Why do you think the shop has such a limited selection?

_____

_____

2. Why doesn't the shopkeeper have a copy of *Jane Eyre*?

_____

_____

3. Why is Carly so upset at the end of chapter 10?

_____

_____

4. Why is it so difficult for the Brontë sisters to express themselves?

_____

_____

5. Why does Emily call Carly "Miss Impertinence"?

_____

_____

6. What are "domestic arts"?

_____

7. How did you feel when Carly stood up to Branwell?

_____

_____

8. Describe how Carly's point of view and words to the Brontë sisters influenced their actions, and events that are unfolding.

_____

_____

_____

Activities:

In this chapter, the Brontë sisters are considering doing something groundbreaking. Not only are they out to "prove that a truly Christian heroine need be neither pretty nor charming to be compelling", but they're also considering sharing their own tragic stories, full of true emotion with the world. In the space below, write a paragraph discussing what effect their choices will have on the course of literature going forward, and why following through with these tasks will require great bravery.

_____

_____

_____

_____

CHAPTER 12

Vocabulary List: chastened, pathos, keen, shirk, malicious, overindulged, convention, agitation

Discussion Questions:

1. When Carly gets back home, why will she have no excuse but to apply to the French Immersion camp?

_____

_____

2. Carly feels insecure that the whole family laughs behind her back for how hard she has to work at French and German. Have you ever felt insecure about a subject or skill? Explain.

_____

_____

_____

_____

3. How does Carly know that Charlotte has begun writing *Jane Eyre*?

_____

_____

4. Why does Maria fear that the way Charlotte is writing *Jane Eyre* is not good enough?

_____

_____

5. Why do you think Maria is holding back her true feelings as she writes?

_____

_____

6. What does Maria tell Carly that she must do?

_____

_____

Activities:

Reflection: Do you think it is better to "play it safe" and not have people judge, or talk about you? Or, do you think it is better to stay true to yourself, no matter what the consequence may be?

CHAPTER 13 and CHAPTER 14

Vocabulary List: fetid, scarcely, doggedly, rotund, tumultuous, tincture, pestilential, beseechingly

Discussion Questions:

1. What does Carly mean when she says, "Nineteenth-century England was way better on paper than in real life"? _____

_____

2. Who arrives on horseback to rescue Carly? _____

3. What is the medical procedure "bleeding", **and** why doesn't Carly want Dr. Bruening to bleed her?

_____

_____

4. While Charlotte watches over Carly, as she lay in bed ill, who is she reminded of?

_____

5. What does Carly ask Charlotte to promise her?

_____

Activities:

Science Connection: Research the weather in Juneau, Alaska. Find out why a whole week of school is devoted to learning survival skills, and make a list of what those skills are.

CHAPTER 15 and CHAPTER 16

Vocabulary List: uncanny, efficacious, compulsion, scalding, tremulously, cosseting, lucid, querulous, prevalent, rueful, gruel, deciphering, irksome, convalescence, haltingly, amended

Discussion Questions:

1. What is the only thing that calms Carly while she is ill?

_____

2. What is the name of the book that Emily is writing? ___

3. Who is Elizabeth? _____

4. What caused the death of Maria and Elizabeth? _____

_____

5. When Carly finished reading the final pages of Jane Eyre, Maria appeared and said, Thank you Carly- you have freed us, and so you have freed yourself." Explain how Carly freed the Brontë sisters.

_____

_____

_____

6. When Carly returned to the bookstore, and was explaining to Francesca that she had gone "into a book", she could hardly contain her excitement when sharing the details of the adventure she'd been on. Have you ever had a book affect you in that way? Explain.

_____

_____

_____

_____

7. How did Carly inspire, or help, the Brontë sisters?

_____

_____

_____

How did the Brontë sisters inspire, or help, Carly?

_____

_____

_____

Have you ever had a literary character, or author, inspire, or help, you in your life? If so, how?

_____

_____

_____

8. Which Brontë sister's book do you most want to read: Jane Eyre by Charlotte Brontë, Wuthering Heights by Emily Brontë, or Agnes Grey by Anne Brontë?

Activities:

The Brontë sisters were very intelligent and forward thinking for their time, to consider opening their own school, traveling abroad to Brussels, becoming authors, and doing such things as revolutionizing the female character and expressing true feelings and tragedy in their writings. Research what life was like for women in 1846: what their roles were, what opportunities existed or did not exist for them, what rights they did or did not have. Then, write an essay on the extraordinary lives and accomplishments of the Brontë sisters.

For more educational and character-building activities, visit beanoblekid.org

Common Core Curriculum Standards met by this Reading Guide:

Grade 3:

CCSS.ELA-LITERACY.RL.3.1 Ask and answer questions to demonstrate understanding of a text, referring explicitly to the text as the basis for the answers.
CCSS.ELA-LITERACY.RL.3.3 Describe characters in a story (e.g., their traits, motivations, or feelings) and explain how their actions contribute to the sequence of events
CCSS.ELA-LITERACY.RL.3.4 Determine the meaning of words and phrases as they are used in a text, distinguishing literal from nonliteral language.
CCSS.ELA-LITERACY.RL.3.6 Distinguish their own point of view from that of the narrator or those of the characters.
CCSS.ELA-LITERACY.L.3.4 Determine or clarify the meaning of unknown and multiple-meaning word and phrases based on grade 3 reading and content, choosing flexibly from a range of strategies.
CCSS.ELA-LITERACY.L.3.4.D Use glossaries or beginning dictionaries, both print and digital, to determine or clarify the precise meaning of key words and phrases.
CCSS.ELA-LITERACY.L.3.5 Demonstrate understanding of figurative language, word relationships and nuances in word meanings.
CCSS.ELA-LITERACY.SL.3.1 Engage effectively in a range of collaborative discussions (one-on-one, in groups, and teacher-led) with diverse partners on grade 3 topics and texts, building on others' ideas and expressing their own clearly.
CCSS.ELA-LITERACY.SL.3.4 Report on a topic or text, tell a story, or recount an experience with appropriate facts and relevant, descriptive details, speaking clearly at an understandable pace.
CCSS.ELA-Literacy.W.3.7 Conduct short research projects that build knowledge about a topic.

Grade 4:

CCSS.ELA-LITERACY.RL.4.1 Refer to details and examples in a text when explaining what the text says explicitly and when drawing inferences from the text.
CCSS.ELA-LITERACY.RL.4.2 Determine a theme of a story, drama, or poem from details in the text; summarize the text.
CCSS.ELA-LITERACY.RL.4.3 Describe in depth a character, setting, or event in a story or drama, drawing on specific details in the text (e.g., a character's thoughts, words, or actions).
CCSS.ELA-LITERACY.RL.4.4 Determine the meaning of words and phrases as they are used in a text, including those that allude to significant characters found in mythology (e.g., Herculean).
CCSS.ELA-LITERACY.L.4.4 Determine or clarify the meaning of unknown and multiple-meaning words and phrases based on grade 4 reading and content, choosing flexibly from a range of strategies.
CCSS.ELA-LITERACY.L.4.4.a Use context (e.g., definitions, examples, or restatements in text) as a clue to the meaning of a word or phrase.
CCSS.ELA-LITERACY.L.4.4.c Consult reference materials (e.g., dictionaries, glossaries, thesauruses), both print and digital, to find the pronunciation and determine or clarify the precise meaning of key words and phrases.
CCSS.ELA-LITERACY.SL.4.1 Engage effectively in a range of collaborative discussions (one-on-one, in groups, and teacher-led) with diverse partners on grade 4 topics and texts, building on others' ideas and expressing their own clearly.
CCSS.ELA-LITERACY.SL.4.4 Report on a topic or text, tell a story, or recount an experience in an organized manner, using appropriate facts and relevant, descriptive details to support main ideas or themes; speak clearly at an understandable pace.
CCSS.ELA-LITERACY.W.4.2 Write informative/explanatory texts to examine a topic and convey ideas and information clearly.

Grade 5:

CCSS.ELA-LITERACY.RL.5.2
Determine a theme of a story, drama, or poem from details in the text, including how characters in a story or drama respond to challenges or how the speaker in a poem reflects upon a topic; summarize the text.

CCSS.ELA-LITERACY.RL.5.3
Compare and contrast two or more characters, settings, or events in a story or drama, drawing on specific details in the text (e.g., how characters interact).

CCSS.ELA-LITERACY.RL.5.4
Determine the meaning of words and phrases as they are used in a text, including figurative language such as metaphors and similes.

CCSS.ELA-LITERACY.L.5.4
Determine or clarify the meaning of unknown and multiple-meaning words and phrases based on grade 5 reading and content, choosing flexibly from a range of strategies.

CCSS.ELA-LITERACY.L.5.4.c
Consult reference materials (e.g., dictionaries, glossaries, thesauruses), both print and digital, to find the pronunciation and determine or clarify the precise meaning of key words and phrases.

CCSS.ELA-LITERACY.L.5.5
Demonstrate understanding of figurative language, word relationships, and nuances in word meanings.

CCSS.ELA-LITERACY.L.5.5.a
Interpret figurative language, including similes and metaphors, in context.

CCSS.ELA-LITERACY.SL.5.1
Engage effectively in a range of collaborative discussions (one-on-one, in groups, and teacher-led) with diverse partners on grade 5 topics and texts, building on others' ideas and expressing their own clearly.

CCSS.ELA-LITERACY.SL.5.4
Report on a topic or text or present an opinion, sequencing ideas logically and using appropriate facts and relevant, descriptive details to support main ideas or themes; speak clearly at an understandable pace.

CCSS.ELA-LITERACY.SL.5.5
Include multimedia components (e.g., graphics, sound) and visual displays in presentations when appropriate to enhance the development of main ideas or themes.

CCSS.ELA-LITERACY.W.5.2
Write informative/explanatory texts to examine a topic and convey ideas and information clearly.

CCSS.ELA-LITERACY.W.5.7
Conduct short research projects that use several sources to build knowledge through investigation of different aspects of a topic.

CCSS.ELA-LITERACY.W.5.9
Draw evidence from literary or informational texts to support analysis, reflection, and research.

CCSS.ELA-LITERACY.W.5.9.a
Apply grade 5 Reading standards to literature (e.g., "Compare and contrast two or more characters, settings, or events in a story or a drama, drawing on specific details in the text [e.g., how characters interact]").

Authors: National Governors Association Center for Best Practices, Council of Chief State School Officers

Title: Common Core State Standards (Reading: Literature, Grades 3-6)

Publisher: National Governors Association Center for Best Practices, Council of Chief State School Officers, Washington D.C.
Copyright Date: 2010

CPSIA information can be obtained at www.ICGtesting.com
Printed in the USA
LVOW01s1719310714

396924LV00004B/926/P